PRAISE FOR *SANCTUARY LIGHT*

"This children's book is next level. Nicole Parker has done something remarkable in *Sanctuary Light*. She has achieved a powerful combination of simplicity and depth, while simultaneously creating a delightful story that keeps the reader turning pages to find out what's next. This is a children's book that adults will be secretly reading after the kids are in bed."

—Ty Gibson
Author, Co-director of *Light Bearers* and Senior Pastor of Storyline Adventist Church

"A delightful story - creatively and sensitively told - that leads children to a deep appreciation of the greatest story ever told. *Sanctuary Light* brings the gospel alive in a way that reaches the heart, meaningfully and graciously told."

—John Bradshaw
Speaker/Director, *It Is Written*

"Do you want children to see the Sanctuary message as relevant, practical, and beautiful? This book will win them over, educate them, and endear them to a loving God. And it will do the same for you! As a mental health professional, a mother, and a student of the Bible, I couldn't place a better tool in your hands."

—Jennifer Schwirzer, LPC
Author, Counselor, Director of Abide Counseling Network

"Nicole Parker uses the vehicle of a story about a family to highlight practical lessons from the Old Testament Sanctuary in a way that children can understand, and in doing so, she shows the spiritual depth and relevance of the Sanctuary and its services for Christians today. She emphasizes that the heart of the Sanctuary message was the Lord's call for His people to trust Him completely and surrender everything to Him. This is a book worth reading—and rereading—to our children."

—Dr. Greg A. King
Dean, School of Religion, Southern Adventist University

"Our family loved this book! Written in a heartwarming, exciting style, it's a page-turner that is set in the time of the Israelites, telling the story of children who had the literal Sanctuary in their camp. It traces their experience with life, forgiveness, the Sanctuary, and God. It explains the plan of salvation in a way that children can readily understand, using the Bible's sandbox illustration—the Sanctuary."

—Bill Krick
Pacific Union Literature Ministries Director

"*Sanctuary Light* entranced our entire family. My homeschooled children are 6 and 8 years old, and begged for a chapter every night. This story inspired deeper and richer conversations about God's love than any other resource we have ever used."

—Sarah McDugal
Author, Speaker, Abuse Recovery Coach

"*Sanctuary Light* came as a timely blessing to our family. My children (ages 9, 11, and 14) each came to me to discuss aspects of the Sanctuary and the meaning of the gospel that they had newly understood from reading this story. Even as an adult, I gleaned fresh and inspiring insight from this wonderful book!"

—Lindsey Pitts, MSW
Homeschooling Mom

"Even though this book was written for children, it has revolutionized the way I understand the Sanctuary and the judgment. I used to feel fear and intimidation when I thought about the Sanctuary message, but now I feel such joy and peace! I have shared it with several of my friends here at the university and at home, and they said the same thing. Because it was not a textbook or an analysis, it was so easy to understand and fun to read!"

—Karen Sardar
Nursing Student, Southern Adventist University

Sanctuary Light

NICOLE PARKER

· BOOK 7 ·
TALES OF THE EXODUS SERIES
www.TalesoftheExodus.com

ISBN 978-1981289332

Illustrated by Adel Arrabito Torres.
Cover art by Adel Arrabito Torres and Christin Smolinski.
Typesetting by Hanna Burks.

Dedicated to my wonderful, supportive husband Alan,
who shows me God's love every day,

———

And to our four precious children:
Skyler, our giggler and snuggler,
Seth, our prankster and philosopher,
Anaya, our dreamer and writer,
and Anya, our conqueror and belly laugher,
our surprise gift from Ukraine.

We love each one of you more than words can express.

———

Remember the message of the Sanctuary:
God is always for you, never against you—
and so are Daddy and I.

ACKNOWLEDGMENTS

I owe an abundant debt of thanks to Dr. Jirí Moskala for sharing his wisdom and insights in Sanctuary class as well as afterward, when he read through my manuscript.

I am also immensely grateful to my friends Bill and Heather Krick for urging me to publish this book, and to Lindsey Pitts, Sarah McDugal, Stephanie Livergood (and all of their children!) and so many others who read the manuscript and gave me valuable insights and editing suggestions.

Especially, I thank God for His immeasurable love and goodness, as expressed in the beautiful message of the Sanctuary. I pray this book blesses every reader as much as the study of the Sanctuary has blessed me.

PREFACE

I was skeptical when Dr. Jirí Moskala stated at the beginning of my week-long seminary intensive class on the Sanctuary, "This doctrine is the most important pillar of the Seventh-day Adventist faith!" *I know the Sanctuary so well I could already teach this class myself*, I thought. After all, I had taken an entire class on the Sanctuary before, read numerous books, and could draw a model of the Sanctuary easily. In my pride, I had no idea what awaited me.

My understanding of the Sanctuary was transformed forever that week. Dr. Moskala's beautiful, compelling presentation of the glorious Sanctuary message answered so many questions I hadn't even realized lingered in my heart. By the end of the week, I literally drove home watching cars on the other side of the freeway and thinking, "I wish I could share this message with all of those people—with the whole world!"

Out of fresh and newfound love for the Sanctuary, I wrote this story (initially just for my own children for homeschool), seeking to convey the glorious message of salvation, deliverance and assurance.

I've written the book so it can be read for family worship, studied in homeschool, or just enjoyed as a storybook. For those who want to maximize the benefit, I've added discussion questions at the end of each chapter.

It is my prayer that this message will be as personally transformative for my readers as it has been for me. May you be won by the love of the God who is always for us, never against us, and willing to sacrifice Himself to the uttermost, to save us.

— Nicole Parker

INTRODUCTION

The Sanctuary doctrine is a thrilling biblical teaching with many wonderful and unexpected surprises. It is a vital truth that needs to be transmitted in a very relevant and attractive way to the next generation, our children and grandchildren. Only in this way will our biblical heritage not only survive but flourish in the future and bring ripe fruit. Nicole wonderfully succeeded with this task. I strongly recommend for parents and grandparents to read this book to their posterity. She has made the profound truth simple so that even children can comprehend the story of God's grace for humanity. Nicole brings home in a crystal-clear manner the principal point: God is for us and never against us. He never stops His work on our behalf because He wants to save as many as possible. He yearns for us to know Him in such a way that we are attracted to Him because of His love, grace, and transforming power which will awaken our love for Him, faith in Him, and desire to faithfully follow Him (John 3:16; Romans 8:1; 2 Corinthians 5:17; 1 John 4:19).

To put the complex system of truth, as is the Sanctuary doctrine, in a language that everyone can understand demands an excellent knowledge of the topic, as well as a mastery of the art of communication, and requires a new approach with brilliant ideas. We are usually good in complicating things, but Nicole makes sense of this topic. Asher's and Zara's questions (two main figures in her thrilling story) and their new discoveries will fill the imaginations of our children with vital treasures of truth. I want to commend Nicole for doing it, and I am sure that through reading this dramatized Sanctuary story for children, many adults will also be tremendously blessed.

Today, Jesus Christ is in the heavenly Sanctuary, which has incomprehensible and multidimensional functions, where our all-powerful and great Intercessor daily works for us in that unmeasurable space to completely save us (Romans 8:34; Hebrews 7:25). To understand the meaning of the doctrine of the Sanctuary for God's people in the past opens the deep fountain of truth that offers us the fresh water of salvation, allowing us to enjoy a rich and victorious life (John 4:10; 7:38).

— Dr. Jirí Moskala, Dean of the Seminary at Andrews University and Professor of Old Testament Exegesis and Theology

TABLE OF CONTENTS

CHAPTER 1

Morning Manna

Asher squirmed under his warm sheepskin coverlet and squinted at the soft light streaming through the tent flap. The sun wasn't up yet—he recognized the orange-yellow glow of the pillar of fire that hovered every night over the camp. Propping himself up on his elbows, he peered over at Zara (ZAH-ra) on the other side of the tent. His little sister was still sound asleep. Judging from the even rhythm of breathing from his parents' bed, he was the only one awake.

Asher crept silently to the doorway, untied the tent flaps, and slipped outside. If he got an early start, maybe he could beat Iru (EE-roo) and the other boys to the best manna heaps. Then after breakfast, he and Zara could continue molding the little mud village they'd been working on all week at the riverbank.

Asher paused in front of his family's tent, gazing reverently toward the Shekinah (sheh-KYE-nah) light glowing from the biggest tent in the center of the huge encampment. In the dark, the brightness blazed through the covering of heavy skins and linen curtains surrounding the tent they called the Sanctuary. He loved getting up early, when the radiance from the center of the settlement flamed the brightest. His heart warmed with peace. *Yahweh is here.* He smiled as he grabbed his manna basket and darted toward the nearby acacia thicket, his favorite manna hunting ground.

The faint rosy pink of dawn brightened the eastern hills as Asher reached the acacia grove, but he could see the manna easily in the golden glow radiating from overhead. The pillar of fire kept them warm on chilly desert nights, and reminded them of *Yahweh's* constant presence. He squatted and set down his basket, cupping both hands and scooping up small clumps of manna.

He worked carefully in the dim light. The clusters were as small as coriander seeds. A few times before, he'd accidentally scooped some sand in with his manna—he didn't want that to happen again!

"Hi, Asher!" Iru's cheerful greeting rang through the cool air. Asher turned to see his friend's familiar brown face beaming at him in the morning light. Iru's brother, Elah (EE-lah), scurried around quietly in the distance, scooping manna into his own basket. "I see we are both up before the sparrows! Where's Zara? Don't tell me you're doing the work all alone today!"

"Everyone in my tent is still asleep. I thought I'd get a head start and surprise Zara." Asher grinned. "Maybe another day it will be her turn."

Iru set down his basket a few feet away and began gathering clusters of manna near some round stones. "Elah and I got up early because we're digging a swimming area along the river today. Want to help?"

"I have to take the sheep out to graze," Asher said regretfully. "I wish I could."

"That's okay—another day." Iru chuckled. "You can come swim in it with us when we finish, anyway!"

Asher filled his basket easily. Zara wouldn't even need to gather today. Before the sun had risen over the mountains to brighten their valley, he straightened proudly and strode back toward the tent, his basket heaped high with mounds of pale manna. Orange and purple streaked across the sky as he reached their tent.

Mama had already started the cooking fire in front of the tent to fry manna cakes. Asher grinned at her, but before handing her his manna basket, he ducked inside the tent. "Guess what I did this morning!" he beamed.

Zara rubbed her eyes and peered up as her brother squatted beside her bed. She sat up and peeked into his basket in astonishment as she threw off her sheepskin covers. "A whole basket? You're a great brother! And I'm starving!"

Giggling, Zara and Asher bounded out of the tent, snatching handfuls of the fresh white sweetness before handing the basket to Mama. Then they raced to the small enclosure nearby to check on the sheep.

The animals stood calmly in their pen, except for two woolly lambs romping just inside the gate. Asher smiled at the sight of them. He leaned over the fence to scratch Cotton's head. Cotton's creamy wool reminded him of the fluffy balls of fuzz all over the ripe

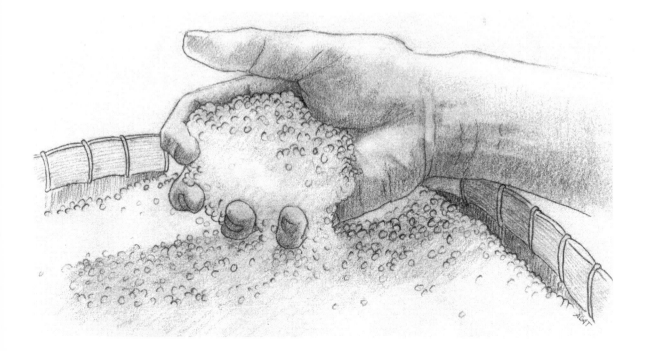

cotton fields of Egypt. He adored his lamb! Zara's black-and-white lamb Daisy frolicked nearby, and Zara laughed with delight at her antics.

Their fun with the lambs was interrupted by the sound of the priest blowing a ram's horn trumpet in the distance. It was time for the morning sacrifice at the big Sanctuary tent at the center of the camp! Asher and Zara raced back to their tent.

Papa waited for them at the tent door. "Thank you for coming right away!" he smiled. Together the family knelt in a circle near the cooking fire while Papa prayed.

"We thank You for Your love and forgiveness," Papa began. "You have brought us out of Egypt and given us a new life here in the wilderness. Thank You for the manna before us, and for the water flowing from the rock. And especially, we thank You for the sacrifice this morning that washes away all our sins, so we may live confidently today in the light of Your presence."

Breakfast was simple but hearty, and Zara helped Mama rinse the dishes while Asher swept the tent floor with a broom made of twigs. "May we go play, Mama?" Zara begged as she wiped the last pottery bowl clean. "Asher and I are making a wonderful little village!"

Mama squinted at the sunlight streaming into the tent. The sun had not yet risen high enough to be obscured by the billowy cloud which shaded them from the blazing desert heat, replacing the pillar of fire during daytime. She smiled. "I suppose you may take an hour or so before the sheep need to graze. But don't get too dirty."

SANCTUARY LIGHT

―――――――

THINKING ABOUT IT

· How would you feel closer to God if you could see the reminder of God's presence in the cloud overhead and the light from the Sanctuary?

· Imagine that every morning, God miraculously provided food for your family in the form of manna. Would you get tired of it? Would you remain thankful every day?

· How can you build your faith that God is with you now, just as surely as He was with Israel in the wilderness camp—even if you can't see miraculous evidence every day?

CHAPTER 2

The Knife

Asher and Zara scampered toward the bank of the river. Upstream, the water rushed in a thundering torrent out of a crack in a huge boulder. He loved to watch the water gush out of the stone. It always reminded him of the day Moses had struck this rock with his rod. With a piercing crack, the boulder had split open and clear, cool water had bubbled out of its depths onto the sandy soil below.

He shivered with awe at the memory. At that moment, he had known without a doubt *Yahweh* was mighty and could take care of them! Every day since then, the fountain continued to pour liquid life as a reminder of *Yahweh's* power and love.

A natural gathering place, the riverbank usually swarmed with people, both friends and strangers. This morning, several children frolicked at the water's edge while their mothers scrubbed clothing and chatted in the clear, shallow water nearby.

Asher and Zara headed toward a secluded nook beside a thicket of scrawny bushes. But someone had beaten them there today. As they approached, two figures jumped up from beside their little mud village and fled—Iru and Elah.

"Iru! Elah!" Asher called, but they did not turn around. Then he saw why. Trampled clay huts littered the riverbank. Iru and Elah had smashed their miniature settlement.

Zara burst into tears, crumpling down onto the bank beside what was left of their little creations. Asher surveyed the destruction in dismay. He turned and raced after the two boys. "You broke our houses!" he shouted. "Come back here!"

The boys didn't even look back.

Asher blinked hot tears out of his eyes. He returned to his sister's side and patted her shoulder. "Maybe we can rebuild them. Look, they didn't break this house."

"They didn't even care," Zara sobbed. "Look at my sheep pen! It's ruined." She gathered snapped twigs, then dropped them in a despairing heap.

Asher's heart smoldered with anger. All of their work, gone! They had been having such fun. It had been nearly finished! He had hoped to show the village to Mama and Papa tonight.

He paced down the bank. "I can't believe Iru was so mean," he muttered, gritting his teeth. "We never did anything to him!"

"Maybe he didn't know it was our village."

"Maybe not," Asher admitted, "but he shouldn't have just destroyed it! Now, all of our work is gone. We might as well go home for now." He helped his sister to her feet.

As they turned to leave, Asher spotted something odd beneath the bushes near their mud city. "Hey, look!" He stooped and picked up a brown goatskin case. He twisted the strap off and slipped a gleaming blade out of the small sheath.

"I wonder whose that is!" Zara's mouth fell open. She wiped away her tears. "Someone must have brought it from Egypt."

"I know whose it is," scowled Asher. "Iru showed it to me last week. His uncle gave it to him as a present. It is very special—knives like this are rare."

"Their tent isn't far from ours." Zara sniffled and crossed her arms over her chest. "Except I don't feel like talking to him right now."

"Neither do I." Asher cradled the little knife in his hand and looked at it, then at his sister. "Let's keep it—for now, anyway."

Zara's eyes widened. "But—isn't that stealing?"

"Didn't they steal our village?" Asher strode toward their tent without waiting for an answer.

His anger burned all day as he watched the sheep graze. *How dare they ruin our village and then run away when we caught them! I thought Iru was my best friend—but not anymore!* He consoled himself by whittling some small sticks with Iru's knife. The shavings flew off easily, satisfying his urge to destroy something.

After sharpening a few soft branches, he decided to try making something useful. He chose an acacia rod and began whittling the hard wood. It was difficult work, but over the next hour, the twisted stick began to shine. *With a little practice,* he thought, *I could make some neat things! And out here every day with the sheep, all I have is time.* With nothing to do but gather sticks for the fire during the day, why couldn't he keep the knife? Maybe *Yahweh* had made Iru drop it. *After Iru destroyed our village, I deserve his knife anyway!*

As Asher returned home with the sheep that evening, the ram's horn trumpet sounded through the warm air. He dropped to his knees for a quick prayer of rededication—then paused.

He opened his hand and gazed at Iru's knife. His mind flashed to the Ten Commandment stones. Instinctively, he lifted his eyes in the direction of the Sanctuary. There in the Most Holy Place, under the blazing glory and the Mercy Seat, he imagined the smooth Ten Commandment stones bearing their silent testimony to the holiness of *Yahweh's* law. *You must not steal.*

Kneeling in the dust, Asher heard the last ringing blast of the ram's horn trumpet, reminding all of Israel to prepare their hearts for the evening sacrifice. *But the blood only covers repented and confessed sins,* he thought, *a chill running up his spine. If I keep the knife, my sins won't be covered!*

For several minutes, he knelt, rooted in place, hovering between the choice of good or evil. He looked toward the Sanctuary, then down at the coveted knife. He tried to imagine walking to Iru's tent and handing him the knife. He could almost see Iru's smug, smirking face after he'd smashed the mud village. Fresh anger jolted through him. *No, I can't. I just can't. And it wouldn't be fair! I'll just keep it for a little while. Maybe I can return it tomorrow.*

When he arrived back at his family's tent, Asher paused outside. He quickly glanced around—no one was nearby. He crouched next to a corner of the tent and scooped away the sandy soil. Then he slipped the knife in the hole and heaped the earth back. He placed a rock over the spot, smoothed a few leaves over it, and stood up. No one would

THE KNIFE

know the knife was even there.

His heart pounded in his chest. His mouth felt dry. He led the sheep to their pen and secured the latch behind them, pausing to scratch Cotton's head with trembling fingers.

Asher had just stolen Iru's knife.

THINKING ABOUT IT

· Imagine you were in a desert with your family and friends, afraid you might die of thirst. Then God miraculously made fresh water come out of a rock. How would you feel? How can you build your faith on the story of this miracle, even if you weren't there to see it?

· Should Asher and Zara have assumed the worst about Iru and Elah running away from the trampled mud village? How could they have handled the situation differently?

· How do you think God wants our morning and evening worship time to be like the morning and evening sacrifice time in the Israelite camp?

CHAPTER 3

The Law of Love

"Did you take Iru's knife back?" asked Zara as soon as Asher entered the tent.

Trapped, he gazed into her trusting brown eyes, then looked up to see his mother also watching him. "I-I saw him while I was herding the sheep, so I gave it to him," he mumbled.

He was surprised at his own boldness. He had never intentionally lied before. *Two commandments broken now!* Horror flashed in his heart. He turned quickly and fumbled around beside his sheepskin bed. He needed a distraction. "Look, Zara, I found these pretty pebbles the other day and thought we could add them to our village. Do you want to start working on it again?"

Zara nodded. She sprang up from the floor where she was helping spin fluffy wool into stringy yarn. "Oh, yes! May we, Mama?"

"We need to finish supper preparation first," Mama chided, handing Zara her small kneading trough full of manna dough. "Will you finish winding the yarn onto a spool, Asher?"

Zara and Mama kneaded dough as he bent over the yarn. His heart thudded so loudly in his ears, he was sure Mama would hear it. *That was close!* he thought. *I can't believe I lied. So easily, too!*

As he wound the newly spun yarn onto the wooden spool, he noticed for the first time how the stick had been smoothed first with something sharp. *I could easily make spools like this for Mama.* Then his stomach tightened as he remembered. He couldn't show anyone anything he'd made with the stolen knife! They would ask him questions, and he didn't have good answers. *I didn't even bring home any sticks tonight, because I carved all of them with the knife. I guess I already started living a lie before I even got home.*

Sobered, he finished rolling the yarn onto the smooth stick, then stowed the spool of yarn in Mama's weaving basket. He wondered how much of his life was going to be affected by this choice. *Keeping the knife might be harder than I thought.*

At supper an hour later, Zara chattered nonstop. Usually Asher welcomed the opportunity to talk after a long day alone with the sheep, but today he felt irritated at the constant babble.

"Papa," Zara said suddenly, "why do we have to sacrifice lambs? I don't understand why—" she paused in reverence before whispering the holy Name, "why *Yahweh* would want anything to die."

Papa slowly finished chewing his mouthful of manna cake before answering. "That is a hard question, Zara, one many people have asked. Especially here in the wilderness, our flocks are precious. We can't just buy new animals at an Egyptian market. Of course, we do not have to sacrifice animals often—only when we engage in willful sins or break commandments. And for some intentional sins, such as murder or unfaithfulness to a husband or wife, no sacrifice in our Sanctuary can cover them."

"You mean *Yahweh* can't forgive those sins?" Zara asked, eyes widening in horror.

"No, no," Papa corrected. "*Yahweh* can forgive any sins which are sincerely repented and confessed. But these sins must be dealt with severely in our camp. In order to commit such a sin, a person must have dedicated their heart to the persistent pursuit of evil for a long time."

"So there are three kinds of sins," Zara pondered aloud. "Smaller ones covered by morning and evening sacrifices, intentional sins breaking *Yahweh's* law which require personal sacrifices, and sins so terrible that no sacrifice at our Sanctuary can cover them."

"That's correct." Papa patted her on the head. "You are learning fast! Remember, *Yahweh* always forgives truly repentant hearts. The reason some sins cannot be covered by an animal sacrifice in our Sanctuary is because we cannot allow such sin to continue in our camp. Also, because *Yahweh* knows we must take these sins very seriously. To allow such sins to be taken lightly would destroy our nation."

"There is no such thing as a small sin, Zara," Mama pointed out. "All sin starts with things we like to consider small. Our sinful hearts are natural fountains of pride and unbelief, the two great sins at the root of all other sinful thoughts and behaviors. Unbelief destroys our ability to love *Yahweh.* When we stop trusting His amazing love for us and others, we exalt ourselves instead of loving and lifting up one another." Mama shook her head sadly, then continued. "But some sins are especially damaging to relationships. Allowing very serious sins like adultery and murder to happen in our camp without a severe penalty would lead to tremendous wickedness and crime. We would become like the pagan nations around us." Mama handed each of the children another manna cake and dusted the crumbs from the empty wooden serving platter into the fire. "If murderers could continue living with freedom in our camp, everyone else would live in constant terror. How could we feel secure in our tent? Unlike Egypt, we don't have a prison."

"Someday," Papa added, "the Messiah's sacrifice will be big enough to cover all of those terrible sins. *Yahweh* can forgive any sin, if the sinner repents. But people who do those things have spent much time planning and rejecting *Yahweh's* voice. They must be removed from relationships with other people because those sinful choices harm others so much. Those who commit such sins have ignored *Yahweh's* voice so persistently, they cannot be trusted anymore."

"That makes sense." Zara bit off a morsel of manna cake and savored it thoughtfully. "But then, why does *Yahweh* ask for the morning and evening sacrifices?" Her small face puckered in a troubled frown. "It seems like such a waste to kill so many animals. Why can't He forgive us without anything dying?"

Mama knelt beside the cooking fire and stirred it with a stick, sending a shower of sparks skyward. "Zara, even when we commit no willful violations of the Ten Commandment law, we are still sinners in desperate need of grace to cover us." Mama's dark eyes sparkled in the dancing firelight. "We selfishly take the biggest manna cake for ourselves. We are sometimes careless with our words. Our thoughts wander to places they shouldn't.

These are not reflections of loving-kindness, the character of *Yahweh*."

Papa straightened, walked over, and sat down between Zara and Asher, putting one arm around each of them. "All sin begins with destroying relationship. That is the very definition of sin. If we break relationship with *Yahweh*, the brokenness bleeds into the rest of our lives, breaking our relationships with others, too."

"Everywhere sin touches, it poisons and destroys loving connection," Mama added sadly. "Sinful actions toward others are never the true problem—they are the fruit, the result, of what has already happened in the heart."

"Then why are the Ten Commandments all about actions?" Asher asked. "It seems like they should just talk about relationships, if that's all that matters."

"When you think more deeply about the commandments, all of them are about relationships," Papa corrected gently. "The first four are about loving Him. The last six are about loving others. But it is hard for sinners to understand how to live in love. So *Yahweh* gave us some basic rules to live by. Obeying them helps us learn how to love Him and others.

"The morning and evening sacrifices remind us to tune our hearts at least twice a day to harmony with *Yahweh*," Papa continued. He gave each of them a squeeze. "And they remind us to repent if there are ways we have not surrendered to Him or reflected His loving-kindness during the day. That is why we pause twice a day to think and pray. The Ten Commandments remind us to love *Yahweh* and to love others—and all of us have far to go in both of those areas, to become like Him."

"So, the morning and evening sacrifices are to remind us, no matter how good we may behave, that we still need grace to cover us every day?" Zara peered up at Papa as she snuggled under his bearded chin.

"Yes, that's an important part of their purpose. And there are other reasons, too." Papa smiled, patting Zara's dark curls. He held out both hands to Asher and Zara to help them up. "But that's probably all these two tired little heads can absorb. Time for bed! We can talk another day."

THE LAW OF LOVE

———

THINKING ABOUT IT

· How did Asher's decision to steal the knife (even if he thought it was temporary) lead to breaking other commandments? Can you think of any other commandments he broke when he kept the knife?

· Did the Israelites have to sacrifice a lamb every time they sinned?

· Do we need grace to cover us every day, even when we cannot think of something specific we have done wrong? How did the morning and evening sacrifices remind Israel of this?

CHAPTER 4

The Sanctuary

"Mama, how do you and Papa know so much about the Sanctuary?" Zara asked as she munched on a manna wafer at breakfast the next morning. "You can't go inside to see the Holy Place and Most Holy Place, and neither you nor Papa can even read. How can you understand Moses' writings about it?"

"Even if they could read," Asher retorted, "what difference would it make? Nobody has expensive parchment paper for writing even small things, never mind all of Moses' writings."

"Speak kindly, Asher," Mama said gently. "What you say is true, my daughter." Asher could hear the sadness in Mama's voice. She parted Zara's hair with the sharp edge of a comb made of bone. "Growing up in slavery has caused Papa and me—and all of Israel—great disadvantages. We hope you and Asher will have many opportunities we do not have. But thankfully," Mama said, her voice dropping to a reverent whisper before she said the holy Name, "*Yahweh* has given Moses instructions on how to help us learn the holy requirements. The Ten Commandments are in the Ark of the Covenant in the Most Holy Place. The other laws *Yahweh* gave Moses are stored with the Ark as well, only on the side of it. The Ark is in a place where none of us can go—not even the priests. Only the High Priest can go into the Most Holy Place, and that is only once a year on the Day of Atonement. But every seven years all of Israel gathers to hear both the commandments and the laws of Moses read aloud. We can go to the Sanctuary and ask questions from those who are trained, so they can teach us, too."

"In fact," Papa pointed out, "just before He gave us the Ten Commandments, *Yahweh* told us He wanted us to be a kingdom of priests, a holy nation to represent Him to all of the surrounding nations. At that time, He called all of us to be priests." He paused sadly. "But perhaps because so many people hardened their hearts and worshiped the golden calf, He had to set up this secondary system to teach us more of what it means to be a holy nation first." He smiled. "Someday, perhaps after Messiah comes and reveals a more perfect way, all of *Yahweh's* people will be priests. Maybe all of our nation will be a light to the Canaanites, the Egyptians—the whole world! I'm sure we can't imagine what He has planned, but it is glorious, this promised kingdom of priests."

"The priests teach others about the laws of *Yahweh*," Mama said. "They represent, by their dress and actions, what Messiah will do someday. And they mediate for others. Perhaps someday when His character is more fully revealed through all of His people, as a kingdom of priests, we will all teach, mediate and show the rest of the world the loving character of *Yahweh*!"

"It would be amazing to be a priest," Asher said. "I wish I could go into the Holy Place just once!"

"That important work is now reserved only for the men of the tribe of Levi, between the ages of 30 and 50 years old, who are not handicapped in any way," Papa said. "They don't need many priests to do such a small amount of work. And I'm not sure you would enjoy it much. Most of their work is about sacrificing animals."

"That's what is so hard for me to understand..." Zara's voice trailed off. Asher sensed she was searching for words to express a deep struggle in her heart. "I still don't see why we have to kill lambs. I love Daisy so much! Why can't we be forgiven some other way? Why does *Yahweh* need the blood of a sacrifice to forgive us?"

"Do we have to keep talking about sacrifices?" Asher grumbled.

He saw Papa and Mama exchange worried glances. "My son," Papa said, "don't you remember *Yahweh's* admonition to us? We are to talk about these lessons when we sit down, when we go for walks together—all the time, so the lessons can be ingrained in our hearts. Doesn't it worry you that you don't want to talk about spiritual things?"

"Sorry, Papa." Asher nodded. *Cherishing this sin is already changing me,* he thought, suddenly frightened. "But...most other families don't talk like this all the time."

"Sadly, many children in Israel are growing up without thinking much about the sacrificial system," Papa admitted. "But that's part of why *Yahweh* had to include something as disturbing as the death of animals. A less shocking system would not make us pay attention to the deadliness of sin. Sheep, goats and other animals are precious, and we are to be kind and thoughtful toward them. The very fact that *Yahweh* would ask us to kill them shows how seriously we need to take our problem with sin."

"Personally, I'm grateful we don't have to sacrifice animals ourselves often." Mama wound a leather strap tightly around the braid she had finished on one side of Zara's head. "Almost all of our sins are covered by the morning and evening sacrifices."

"But why do we even need those?" Zara spun around to look up at Mama. Mama tugged her braid gently to turn her head back before beginning the process of taming her curls for the second braid.

Papa smiled. "The morning and evening sacrifices remind us we have not become perfectly loving toward *Yahweh* and others, as the law commands. There will always be room to grow in becoming more loving! Being righteous is not about behavior. It's about the heart. It's about a new way of thinking—of living by faith, of seeking a loving, growing relationship with *Yahweh* and others.

"As we realize our sinfulness," Papa continued, "in faith and love, we also understand the need for the righteousness which covers us through those sacrifices. We are humbled as we realize how much *Yahweh* has forgiven us. Our gratefulness for grace leads us to live in constant eagerness to learn any new way we can please *Yahweh*."

"The morning and evening sacrifices also comfort us with the promise *Yahweh* has already provided," Mama assured Zara. "He wants us to live joyfully, not in constant fear, worrying whether we need to kill a lamb to be safe! *Yahweh* wants us to recognize our sinfulness, but He also wants His people to live in confidence. We can have peace,

assurance that if we have no known sin holding our hearts back, we are covered by the sacrifice of the coming Messiah."

A peaceful smile softened Papa's face as he glanced toward the holy place of worship at the center of the camp. "Of course, you know this Sanctuary tent is only symbolic. Its services represent what *Yahweh* showed Moses is happening in heaven. We cannot begin to understand everything regarding the services of the heavenly Sanctuary, for they are certainly not sacrificing lambs there!" He tousled Asher's dark curls. "I'm sure it is immeasurably grander and more beautiful than anything here on earth. But still...I like to think of our Sanctuary as a glimpse of heavenly glory."

"We know the most important thing," Mama added. She wrapped the second leather strap around Zara's boisterous braid. "What is happening in the sanctuary of our hearts matters most. Full surrender includes eagerness to live by anything *Yahweh* shows us. When we have this attitude in our hearts, unless we are willfully clinging to sin, we are safe."

"I was thinking last night about how unsafe I felt our last day in Egypt." Zara shuddered. "Remember the day before the Passover? Right up until Papa painted the doorposts, I was afraid Asher would die."

"But when the blood was on the doorposts, we knew by faith we were safe inside our home," Mama reminded her. "Can you see why *Yahweh* provides the symbolic system of the Sanctuary? Once Papa had painted the blood on the doorposts, we felt secure inside our house because we had obeyed *Yahweh's* instructions, and we trusted His promise."

"*Yahweh* knows how weak our faith can be, and how we need symbols to help us understand salvation," Papa said. "When we surrender ourselves to Him and seek His face, the Messiah's future sacrifice already covers us here in our tent, just as it did in our house in Egypt."

"What if we break a commandment on purpose?" Asher's heart went cold with fear as the question tumbled out, but the words were spoken before he could stop them.

"Then we must repent and sacrifice a lamb." Papa cast a troubled glance at him. "A lamb without spot or blemish, to represent the Messiah. Because our hearts are hard—because we so easily fall into thinking our sin is not serious. Only when we sacrifice do we realize the depth of the wickedness of violating *Yahweh's* law of love." Papa patted Zara gently on her head as he rose. "Only then do we understand the loving sacrifice the Messiah will someday make to cleanse us from evil."

THINKING ABOUT IT

· What did all of Israel do every seven years to remember and learn the laws of God?

· Was the sacrificial system designed to make people live in fear of being lost if they did not sacrifice a lamb? Or did God want them to live in constant, joyful assurance of salvation? When would people lose their sense of assurance that they were safe?

· What are some reasons God put the lessons of salvation into a symbolic system?

CHAPTER 5

Iru

The sun had nearly set the next day by the time Asher reached the rocky outcropping beside the lower waterfall—his favorite place to get water. He held his goatskin jug under the sparkling cascade, carefully folding his sleeve back from the splashes. The jug was nearly full, and almost too heavy to hold up in the waterfall, when he heard a voice beside him.

"I'm sorry. I didn't realize it was yours."

Asher jumped, sloshing water on the warm stone beneath his feet. He turned to see Iru standing almost at his elbow.

"I was chasing Elah. When I saw the village, he had already trampled it. I was running so fast, I couldn't stop either." Iru's empty jug dangled from his hand, and his lip trembled. He looked miserable. "It was really great. Can I help you rebuild it?"

Asher turned back toward the water, pretending he needed to concentrate on filling

his water jug. He struggled to find the right words. "It's okay," he mumbled finally. "It wasn't that important."

Iru dropped his water jug and helped Asher wrestle his heavy one away from the edge of the waterfall. "You're not mad, then?"

"I guess not." Asher shrugged. "Why did you run away?"

"I just panicked. We were racing to get to the swimming hole. I came back to see what we had stepped on. I was scared. I didn't want you to be mad at me." Iru scuffed his bare toes in the sandy soil. "I came back five minutes later, but you were gone."

The two boys held Iru's goatskin jug under the torrent of water for a few moments. "Is your sister mad?" Iru asked, his voice edged with concern.

"I'll let her know it was an accident," Asher assured him. "She'll understand."

Iru nodded. "Thanks. Yesterday was an awful day for me. I thought you might never play with me again. On top of everything else, remember the knife my uncle gave me? I lost it somewhere yesterday, too. Probably while I was out gathering firewood." Tears brimmed in Iru's eyes.

Asher turned away, his face burning. He fought the impulse to bring relief to his friend. *I can give it to him later and say I found it somewhere,* he thought. *But I haven't finished whittling my stick yet. I'll keep it just a couple more days.*

"Thanks for still being my friend." Iru smiled in relief.

Later that night, Asher burrowed beneath his sheepskin cover, unable to sleep. He couldn't forget Iru's grateful smile. The more he thought about it, the more the knot in his stomach tightened. Long after Zara and his parents were asleep, Asher tossed and turned. He rubbed the tender spot on his finger where whittling with the knife had chafed a blister over the last two days. *I'll get a callus there soon,* he thought. Shocked, he realized that, even though he knew it was wrong, he still planned to keep Iru's knife.

How can I do this to my friend? Shame washed over him. He and Iru had shared so many good times. Their families had been neighbors and close friends in Egypt. Mama and Iru's mother had worked together the whole day before they left, plotting how they would maximize the space in a shared oxcart to bring along as many household goods as possible for both families.

Leaving Egypt, Asher and Iru had walked beside the cart together. They had stared at one another silently at first, grateful they were both still alive. As the reality of the situation dawned on them—they would not be slaves, as their fathers had been—their soberness had bubbled into excitement. They had whooped and shrieked and dashed around, prompting laughing rebukes from their fathers for scaring the sheep.

Asher remembered the night he and Iru had walked through the Red Sea together with the mighty crowd of Israelites. He shivered, recalling the surreal feeling of herding their flock of sheep through the dark, mysterious trench plowed miraculously through the center of the sea. The two of them had briefly escaped from their families to stare at the mighty black walls of water surging on either side of them. He could still remember Iru's awestruck face lit by the cloudy pillar of fire overhead. Gaping with astonished disbelief, Iru had gingerly touched the water with his finger. Laughing in pure joy, he'd dared Asher to do the same.

Now here Asher was, a false friend who had chosen Iru's knife over his friendship. The thought made Asher's stomach churn. *Thanks for still being your friend?* He wondered what Iru would say if he ever found out the truth. With a sigh, he turned over again and tried unsuccessfully to soothe his conscience to sleep.

On a normal sleepless night, Asher would have peeked through the tent flap to gaze at the warm radiance of the Sanctuary. *Yahweh* is here. Just seeing the light of *Yahweh's* presence usually comforted his heart. But tonight, he didn't even want to think about the Sanctuary.

THINKING ABOUT IT

- When we make excuses for our sin, we always go farther into sin than we think we will. How was this true for Asher when he chose to keep the knife?

- Why would looking at the Sanctuary make someone who is intentionally living in sin feel worse?

- Is there any sin you are holding onto by making excuses in your heart right now? Do you want to be set free?

CHAPTER 6

A Hardened Heart

Asher looked around carefully to make sure no one was watching. Then he scraped aside the cool dirt beneath the acacia bush where he had hidden the knife. This new hiding place away from the camp felt much safer than having the knife under the corner of the tent! Replacing the flat brown stone in the hollowed hideout under the bush, he returned to the sheep. He watched the lambs chase one another through the brush, stopping to nibble here and there before abruptly bounding away. *Cotton is getting so big,* he thought with a smile. *I wonder if Mama will be able to weave a coat for me out of his wool when we shear him this year.* Daisy's black-and-white wool would produce a soft gray yarn, but Cotton's creamy white coat stood out in contrast with the browns and greens of the wilderness grasses.

Asher sat down on a sun-warmed stone, chuckling as Cotton and Daisy bounded over to nuzzle him. He reached into his pocket and let them nibble treats from the bag of manna he'd brought along.

Once the lambs had eaten their fill, he pulled out his knife and resumed whittling. He was carving a little reddish-brown statue of Cotton. Despite a couple of small slips with the blade, the model was coming along wonderfully. He longed to proudly show it to his family, but he dared not let anyone know his dark secret.

Other than the yearning to show off his handiwork, life was beginning to feel almost normal again. But he still didn't feel the warmth and security he used to feel when he looked toward the Sanctuary.

The hardest part was enduring morning and evening sacrifice time. When the ram's horn trumpet sounded, Asher had been taught to kneel in prayer and lay any sins on the unseen lamb being sacrificed at the Sanctuary. Now he couldn't. He knew he had not confessed or turned away from his sins. Thinking about the Sanctuary no longer warmed his heart with the realization that *Yahweh* was near. Instead, it made him feel ashamed, sad and far away from *Yahweh*.

The second night after he stole the knife had actually been harder than the first night. After seeing Iru at the waterfall, Asher had admitted to Zara that Iru had apologized and explained about the accidental destruction of their little mud village.

"How do you know he's really sorry?" Zara's lip trembled. "They ran away! It's not fair. They ought to have some punishment."

"Zara, mistakes are covered by the morning and evening sacrifices," Papa reminded her gently.

"If anything," Mama added, "you both have sinned a greater sin yourselves. All day yesterday and today you were thinking evil about Iru and Elah. You have resented them and been unfaithful friends to them. While it's true they should have been more careful and shouldn't have run away," Mama soothed, "you also need to confess your sins of bitterness and evil assumptions so you can be covered by the morning and evening sacrifices." Mama ran her fingers gently over Asher's back.

"We are given so much grace every day, to cover our mistakes, impatient words, and lack of thankfulness," Papa concluded. "We all deserve death. But because of the Sanctuary service, we are given the gift of forgiveness. *Yahweh's* grace covers our sins. When we focus on this, His love fills our hearts and overflows toward others."

Asher had turned away, fearing guilt would be written all over his face. Now he sat on the rock looking at the precious knife gripped in his hand, thinking about Papa's words.

If Papa only knew, he reflected, *he would be so sad. I have taken Iru's knife and I have not repented. I am no longer covered by the morning and evening sacrifices.*

Several times in the past few weeks, he had sneaked to the tent flap when the others were asleep, meditating on the glory shining from the Most Holy Place. In place of the warm glow that had once comforted his soul, he now felt only a cold, aching darkness.

A HARDENED HEART

I'm not covered anymore. Was the knife really worth this? He fought to push the thoughts aside. *Maybe it's not such a big deal.*

Absorbed in his carving, the hours flew as Asher whittled carefully on the tiny wooden lamb. It was late when the rays of the slanting sun blurred his vision. He jumped up from his perch on a rounded stone. Cotton and Daisy were nestled at the base of the rock next to him, but sprang to their feet at his sudden leap.

Asher brushed the dark wood shavings from his robe and smoothed the lamb sculpture with his fingers as he rounded up the sheep. He slipped the knife and the lamb into the folds of the wide belt of cloth around his waist as he followed the herd back toward the camp, gathering firewood absentmindedly. Once again, he tucked his knife and wooden lamb into their dusty hiding place under the flat stone beneath the acacia bush.

THINKING ABOUT IT

· How does persistently holding onto sin gradually lead us to feel about that sin?

· Did sins like bitterness and assuming evil about others require a separate sacrifice to bring atonement, or were they covered by the morning and evening sacrifices?

· Would you want to see the Sanctuary nearby when you knew you had an unconfessed sin standing between you and God?

CHAPTER 7

At-one-ment

"Zara, bring me the salt bag," Mama called toward the tent flap as she stirred the steaming manna stew over the fire pit. "And did we finish off the wild onions?"

"I found more today, Mama!" Asher said, slipping around the corner of the tent. "I took the flock to a new area today." *And found new wood to carve, too,* he thought. He smiled, remembering the soft, honey-colored stick he had discovered and hidden near the new grazing spot. He had begun to wonder if there was a way to sneak his creations into camp and sell them without his family finding out about his knife.

Not *Iru's* knife, not anymore. In the past three weeks, Asher had started thinking of the knife as his own. After a few days of stashing it beneath the tent, he'd grown too fearful of getting caught. Just seeing anyone step near that corner of the tent had flooded him with nervous anxiety. And somehow, he had felt the knife's presence just outside the tent every time the ram's horn trumpet blew for the morning and evening sacrifices.

The new hiding place at the edge of the encampment felt much more secure. Leaving it out in the wilderness quieted his conscience—a little. Now that he knew how easy it was to steal, though, he often worried someone else would find his knife. He didn't like how being a thief and a liar made him suddenly suspicious that everyone else might be deceptive, too.

A thief and a liar. Asher didn't like those words, either. He tried to soften them in his mind, to push the words carved in the commandment stones away. Whenever he looked toward the Sanctuary—especially during the morning and evening sacrifices—he felt the sting of his sin. There the commandment stones lay under the Mercy Seat in the Ark. The foundation of the throne of *Yahweh* was the law, and those who clung to disobedience were condemned. Mercy only covered those whose transgressions were washed away by a sacrifice.

Before, he had often enjoyed slipping over to the tent doorway at night to contemplate the warm light of the Sanctuary. But now even a glance toward the Sanctuary made the blackness in his heart feel deeper. How he hoped he would not feel this way forever!

Sometimes Asher wondered if it was worth carrying this dark secret. But how could he return the knife now? Iru would be angry if he discovered the truth—he was sure of that. And even if he made up a story to cover how he had found the knife, the truth would come out. After all, Mama and Zara knew where and when he had found it. And what was the use of covering one lie with another lie? He would still have unconfessed sin darkening his heart. *No sacrifice would cover an unconfessed sin.*

Asher had already made several excuses to avoid going to the new swimming hole with Iru and Elah. He worried Zara might ask Iru about his knife. Sadly, it seemed he was losing not just a peaceful conscience, but also a cherished friendship.

He slipped into the tent quietly while Zara chattered to Mama outside. Relieved to have the tent to himself, he dusted off his feet and flopped down on the fluffy softness of his sheepskin bed.

"The Sanctuary service was given to teach us about how we are saved from sin," he overheard Mama say, continuing her conversation with Zara. "It is not that the blood of animals is necessary to persuade *Yahweh* to forgive. Rather, it is because we must understand that when sin breaks relationship, death is necessary to bring atonement."

"I know the Day of Atonement is the most important day of the entire year," Zara said. "But what does 'atonement' mean, Mama?"

Asher heard a soft thump as Mama kneaded manna dough in her kneading trough. "Zara," she said softly, "how do I make manna dough?"

Asher cocked his ear toward the open tent flap, puzzled by Mama's sudden change of topic.

"You mix water or milk with manna, of course," Zara answered quickly.

"Yes. But mixing the two into one takes work. It takes time to soften the little balls of manna into a smooth paste we can mold." Asher heard water splash into the shallow wooden trough and knew Mama was illustrating to Zara as she spoke. "Here, Zara, help me."

Asher heard the thump in Zara's smaller kneading trough and imagined her chubby fingers squishing the whitish dough. Both he and Zara loved squeezing dough into shapes to be baked over the fire. For a moment, he felt the impulse to hop up off of his bed and ask for a ball of soft dough to mold, too.

"When we mix the water and manna, we are practicing atonement," Mama explained. "We make the two into one. No longer are they separated by the boundaries of air and space. They come together in at-one-ment!"

"I think I see! So the Day of Atonement is about us becoming one with *Yahweh*!" Zara exclaimed.

"Yes, but it's even more than that," Mama responded. "It's also a day to be sure we are one with each other. Because the law of *Yahweh* is all about relationship with Him and others, the Day of Atonement—and the entire Sanctuary service—is about restoring loving connection with *Yahweh* and others. The great desire of *Yahweh's* heart is for all of us to become one, united by love."

"Then why is a blood sacrifice necessary?"

"Breaking the law of *Yahweh* means breaking relationship with Him and with others. The penalty for that breaking is death. Our union can only be restored through death— because death makes a new life possible."

"Hmmm..." Asher imagined his sister's puzzled frown as she pondered this information. "I still don't really understand."

"I'm not sure any of us understand all about the atonement, Zara, so don't feel badly." Mama laughed. "That's why *Yahweh* has given us the Sanctuary—because at-one-ment is so deep and mysterious! But we can think about the lessons as we make manna cakes, wash clothes, and go about our daily chores. The Sanctuary is always there as a constant reminder to us, that we must contemplate the most important things in life."

"And even a child can grasp the things that are most important when he or she considers the Sanctuary services." Asher jumped in surprise as Papa's voice boomed from right beside Asher's head, as Papa approached around the corner just outside the tent. "Sin separates us from *Yahweh* and from one another. The blood of the lamb represents the sacrifice of the Messiah healing our separation and bringing us back together. Someday, He will come to bring at-one-ment for all of us. Even now, He is using the Sanctuary to restore our relationship with Him and others. Contemplating the lessons helps us understand His love. Because everything about the Sanctuary is about atonement—at-one-ment—becoming one with *Yahweh* and with one another in love."

Asher could hear Mama thumping dough in her trough as she pulled off pieces to roll into small manna balls for supper. "Sin—breaking the law—is really about breaking a loving connection. So it only makes sense that righteousness—keeping the law of *Yahweh*—is all about restoring connection. We can spend our lives contemplating the lessons of the Sanctuary and never get to the bottom of their rich meaning, Zara. But at the same time, what matters is so simple: everything about the Sanctuary teaches us to become one with *Yahweh* and with one another, in love."

One with Yahweh and one another in love. The words rang in Asher's mind as he lay on his sheepskin bed. How he longed to sense that oneness again! Suddenly he felt the weight of his sin keenly. What was it like to feel comforted instead of condemned when he looked at the light of the Sanctuary? He could hardly remember now.

Had it been only a few weeks since he stole the knife? It seemed like so long! So long since he had felt perfect peace settle in his heart after each morning and evening sacrifice, knowing *Yahweh* was giving him another new beginning. So long since he had felt the peaceful assurance of knowing *Yahweh* covered him with grace through the Sanctuary.

AT-ONE-MENT

So long since he had been able to truly enjoy time with Iru—or with his own family. He couldn't even enjoy the new swimming hole!

Taking something forbidden had seemed exciting, but now he longed to go back in time. If he had only known the price of separation his sin would cause, he would have returned the knife immediately. Living with this unconfessed sin was separating him from Iru, Mama, Papa, and Zara.

But worst of all, it was separating him from *Yahweh*.

THINKING ABOUT IT

· What are some ways sin grows bigger and bigger, driving us farther and farther from God and others? Can you think of an example from your own life?

· The law of God is all about relationships—loving God and loving others. What does sin do to relationships?

· If sin's main characteristic is that it breaks relationship with God and others, what does righteousness do?

CHAPTER 8

Caught!

After supper that evening, Papa sat down beside Asher near the dying embers of the fire that had cooked their simple supper. Mama and Zara had slipped away to the river to bathe.

"Asher," Papa said, stirring the coals of the dying fire, "I've noticed you haven't brought much firewood home lately. What have you been doing while herding the sheep?"

Asher's face felt flushed and suddenly hot. He was glad for the gathering darkness. "I'll bring more, Papa. I'm sorry—I guess I've been distracted."

"Is there anything you need to tell me?" Asher could see Papa's concerned face illuminated by the gentle glow of the cloud overhead.

The silence loomed between them while Asher fought the burning desire to tell the truth. "I—I guess not."

Silently, Papa reached into his pocket and pulled out some curled wood shavings. "I found these in Cotton's wool today." He paused. "These wouldn't have anything to do with Iru's lost knife, would they?"

Asher's momentary rush of anger at himself for his foolishness at carving above the lambs' backs dissolved at the look of disappointment in his father's eyes. *How could I have done this to Papa?* Guilt and shame washed over him. Tears spilled down his face and splashed on his lap. He poured out the bitter truth. "I only thought I would keep it for a few days at first. But the longer I lied, the easier it was to keep lying—and the harder it was to imagine telling the truth."

Papa pulled Asher onto his lap and stroked his curls while Asher sobbed out his story. When at last the torrent had ended, Asher wiped his tears and felt peace at last. "I'm going to get the knife and take it to Iru first thing in the morning. I can imagine how relieved he will be."

"I'm afraid I'll have to go with you," Papa whispered. For the first time, Asher looked up and saw the tears on his father's cheeks. "You see, sin breaks trust, and although I forgive you now, it will take work to restore my trust in you. I must make sure you tell Iru the whole truth about what happened. I don't want to risk you being tempted to lie to him about how you found the knife."

Asher nodded, both dreading and looking forward to shedding this terrible burden. "I will tell him everything. I want to make things right. I never want to tell another lie as long as I live."

"That is good," Papa said gently. "But there is also something else we will have to do."

THINKING ABOUT IT

· When is the best time to confess a sin?

· What happens to others' trust in us when we refuse to confess until we are caught? How is trust restored?

· What do you think Asher will have to do to bring both at-one-ment and trust back to his relationships?

CHAPTER 9

The Sacrifice

Morning had arrived—the worst morning of Asher's life. He opened his eyes, blinking for a moment before the terrible realization hit him. He lay frozen in grief under his sheepskin blanket, unable to face reality. But he knew there was no way to escape.

Papa knelt beside his bed. "Come, my son. Let's go."

In the gathering dawn, the two trudged in miserable silence out to the gnarled acacia bush near the edge of the encampment. It took Asher only a few moments to dig up the knife and the treasured lamb sculpture.

He clutched the little wooden figure and buried his face in his father's chest, tears streaming down his cheeks. "Oh, Papa. I'm so sorry!"

His father held him close. Together, they plodded slowly toward Iru's tent. The shocked look of betrayal on Iru's face as he accepted the knife stung Asher's heart. A brief conversation by the tent's door flaps, punctuated with sniffles and ending with a prayer, concluded the first part of the atonement process. Then, with sorrowing hearts but a determined stride, the two figures returned to their tent.

Zara's tear-stained face met them at the door. She and Mama had already gathered manna, so the family sat down silently to eat breakfast. Asher usually loved breakfast, but this morning, everything tasted like dust.

He slipped away from the tent and into the sheep pen. As the ram's horn trumpet announced the morning sacrifice, he buried his face in his lamb's soft wool to muffle his sobs—wool that would never become a robe for him, but whose sacrifice would now cover him in a different way.

After the morning sacrifice and family prayer time, Papa and Asher gently slipped a rope around Cotton's woolly neck. Asher's lamb trotted cheerfully beside him. His heart clenched. He could not stop the tears flowing down his cheeks.

They shuffled between the tents until finally they entered the open ground stretching between the other tents and the Sanctuary tent at the center of the encampment. Asher could smell the smoke of the fragrant incense burning at the Sanctuary. The bittersweet aroma mingled with the scent of scorched animal flesh.

Asher cringed as he looked down at little Cotton. *At least he won't feel that,* he thought. He bent and sadly scratched the soft, fuzzy head of his lamb.

At the Sanctuary, Asher and Papa entered through the curtained doorway in the middle of the eastern side of the cloth outer wall of linen curtain. The altar of burnt offering towered directly in front of them, a sacrifice smoldering at its center. Asher knew his sin offering would soon be burned on the altar, symbolizing the Messiah who would one day pay in blood to take away all sins.

Beyond the large altar, Asher spotted the gleaming brass laver full of shimmering water, ready for the day of cleansing. That's where the priests wash, he thought. The water represented washing clean from sin—which was necessary before the priest could enter the Holy Place with blood for atonement.

A priest met them near the doorway and led them to the place of sacrifice. In hushed

tones, Papa explained the situation. Then Asher placed his trembling hands on Cotton's warm, woolly head. He choked out his confession amid burning tears.

Despite the devastating grief of saying goodbye to his beloved pet, Asher finally sensed relief from the dreadful heaviness of guilt that had weighed on him every time he looked toward the Sanctuary over the past few weeks. The sin would no longer burden his heart like a blanket of darkness, holding him back from forgiveness and peace. Finally, the dreadful sense of dark guilt emptied from his heart. By faith, he grasped the promise of the lamb as never before—that he could be counted righteous even though he had sinned, because someone else would die in his place.

Papa's strong hand closed over Asher's small one on the handle of the knife. With one quick movement, it was over. Cotton's eyes widened in silent shock for a moment. Asher petted his innocent lamb's soft wool as the tears coursed down his cheeks.

Within less than a minute, Cotton collapsed at Asher's feet, quiet and still. Asher continued to stroke his head as the priest held a bowl under the lamb's throat. A few drops of the blood spilling into the bowl splattered onto the hem of Asher's robe. *At least,* he thought, *I will still have Cotton with me in a small way.*

The moments felt like hours. It was all a blur to Asher. He watched as the priest cut off a small piece of flesh, and then placed Cotton's small body on the altar of burnt offering. The priest would eat the small piece of flesh later, to symbolize bearing the sin himself. Asher watched the priest sprinkle some of the blood on the horns of the altar. Then the priest washed his hands and feet and disappeared quietly into the Holy Place of the Sanctuary. Perhaps some of the blood would go into the Holy Place as well; sometimes blood was sprinkled there before the curtain separating the Holy Place from the Most Holy Place. But Asher did not want to watch any more—he buried his face in Papa's chest and sobbed.

Even though he could not see where the priest was going now, Asher knew. He fought his grief, focusing instead on imagining where the priest was now. As the priest entered the Holy Place, Asher could envision the seven-branched candlestick on his left, its beautifully molded flowers and leaves gleaming gold in the flickering light from the olive oil flames. *The Messiah will be the Light of Israel—and of the world.* In the midst of his heartbreak, the thought comforted him.

On the priest's right would be the Table of Shewbread, with its two neat stacks of six round, flat loaves each. *The Bread of Life,* Asher thought. The bread represented *Yahweh's* provision for all their needs, both physical and spiritual. As He nourished them with manna here in the wilderness, so He would take care of them forever, as long as they trusted and obeyed Him.

Directly ahead of the priest as he entered would be the Altar of Incense, with smoldering incense glowing on its surface. Directly behind the altar would be the brilliantly colored curtain of rich red, blue and purple, with sparkling golden angels woven into it. The altar also represented the Messiah, who would bring the prayers of *Yahweh's* followers directly into *Yahweh's* presence. Asher could even imagine the ground in front of the curtain, stained with blood from previous sacrifices, symbolizing the sins committed since the last Day of Atonement. Standing outside snuggled in Papa's arms, Asher sniffed deeply of the bittersweet incense

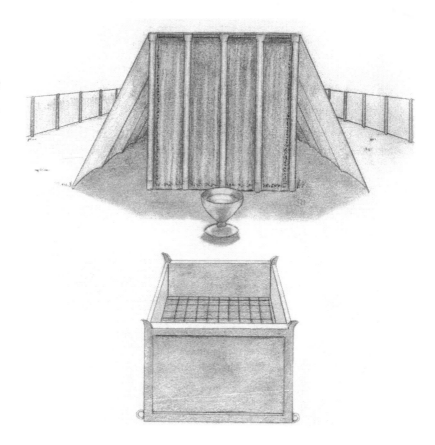

smoke drifting between the drapes of beautifully patterned cloth. He was grateful for the incense, a comforting cover for the smells of blood and burning flesh that lingered in the Sanctuary.

Cotton was gone, his small body burning to ashes, but Asher knew the sin wasn't gone completely—at least, not yet. For now, it would remain symbolically represented on the horns of the Altar of Burnt Offering, and before the curtain of the Most Holy Place, awaiting the Day of Atonement. Thankfully, that day would come soon.

THINKING ABOUT IT

· Whose blood covers your sin when you confess? Is it the same blood that covered the sins of people in the time of Israel?

· Where was Asher's sin symbolically represented as waiting for the Day of Atonement?

· If you had to sacrifice a lamb for your intentional sin, do you think you would take sin more seriously? How much should it matter to us when we break Jesus' heart with our sins?

CHAPTER 10

Assurance

It had been a long day. Though everyone else was in bed, Asher tossed and turned, unable to close his eyes without seeing the heart-wrenching face of his little lamb. Finally, he slipped out of the tent and crouched on the cool, smooth dirt beside the doorway. Gazing toward the glory shining from the Sanctuary, he contemplated what he knew was represented there behind the linen curtain fence—where his sin was now waiting for the Day of Atonement.

Though he could never go inside the Holy Place or the Most Holy Place since he was not a priest, Asher still knew the inside by heart. Papa had used a stick to draw a picture for him in the sand, explaining each symbolic detail. Also, before the dedication of the Sanctuary, Asher and Zara had eagerly watched day after day as the beautiful furniture was molded from the donated precious metals and jewels. They'd admired the careful artistry of the skilled workers making the Sanctuary furnishings. Asher could envision everything inside the Sanctuary in his imagination. Though the Altar of Burnt Offering and the laver of water in the courtyard were made of brass, the spectacular furniture inside the Holy Place and Most Holy Place was made of pure gold.

The sweet-smelling incense smoke symbolized the prayers of *Yahweh's* people coming before the Mercy Seat on top of the Ark of the Covenant, which stood on the other side of the veil. The thought of the smoky symbol comforted him. *I hope my prayers of repentance have already gone into the Most Holy Place with the smoke,* he thought. His sin was now represented in the Sanctuary.

But somehow, even though he had followed all the steps of the sacrificial process, Asher still felt troubled. *How can I know for sure I am forgiven?* After weeks of living with darkness in his heart, feeling a sense of condemnation, it was hard to believe he was really clean now.

"Asher?"

Asher glanced up to see Papa's bearded face in the soft light from the cloud overhead. Papa squatted beside him, then pulled a mat over and sat down on it, wrapping his big, warm arm around Asher's shoulders. Grateful not to be alone, Asher rested his head against Papa's strong chest and listened to the steady *thud-thud* of his heartbeat. Papa's heart is still beating, but Cotton's isn't. Asher glanced toward the sheep pen, wishing he could see Cotton's little nose poking through the fence. He missed his lamb terribly. Tears welled up in his eyes.

"It's been a hard day, my son." Papa's warm whisper melted away some

of the pain in Asher's heart. "But *Yahweh* has taken your sin from you. You're clean, by the blood of the lamb."

Asher leaned against Papa's comforting warmth. "But how can I know for sure, Papa?" he blurted. "I still feel so bad. How can I forgive myself?"

"Son, you will never find within yourself the power to wash away your own sins." Papa rubbed Asher's shoulder. "What you are feeling is a sense of defilement—the need for a forgiveness that can only come from outside of yourself. When sin is a wall between your heart and the heart of *Yahweh*, feeling bad is a good thing. It is called guilt. Guilt is a cry from *Yahweh's* heart straight to yours, saying, 'Sin is standing between us. It is separating your heart from Mine. Let it go so I can cover it—like the Mercy Seat covers the law—and set you free! Then we can be close again.' This is the voice of the Holy One, inviting you to let Him take away your filthy rags."

"But Papa," cried Asher, tears stinging his eyes, "I *have* given it to Him! I've surrendered and sacrificed a lamb. Why do I still feel so awful?"

Papa snuggled him close. "What you are feeling now is not guilt. It feels similar to guilt, but it is shame. And this shame is not a message from *Yahweh*."

Asher wiped his face vigorously on his sleeve. "What's the difference?"

Papa gazed down at him tenderly. "This sense of shame is a message from the accuser. He is lying to

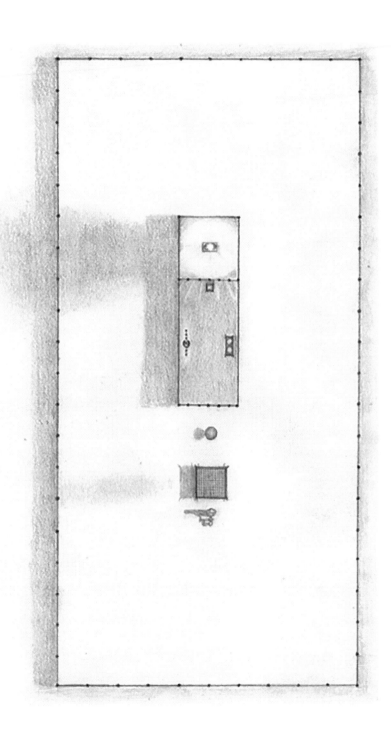

you, telling you that your sin is so great that it goes all the way down to the core of who you are. He is tempting you to unbelief—to doubt that the sacrifice can cover your sin. He wants you to doubt *Yahweh's* loving character." Papa reached down to gently wipe a tear away from Asher's cheek with his rough finger. "If he can succeed in convincing you that you are still dirty—even though you have already confessed and forsaken your sin—then you will fall into sin again."

Asher sat up and looked at Papa, astonished. "But I never want to steal or lie again!" he protested.

"You have learned the bitter results of these transgressions, yes," Papa said. "But your heart is still naturally drawn toward evil is the nature of sinful humanity. Do not cherish this doubt about whether the blood has covered your sins. If you do, you will begin doing good things to persuade *Yahweh* to forgive you—instead of from gratefulness because He has forgiven you."

Asher sniffed as he thought about it. "Is that why I kept praying over and over this afternoon, even after Cotton died, asking *Yahweh* to forgive me?"

Papa nodded. "That is a natural response. Your heart struggled to believe your sin was washed away, so you tried to add to the atonement by punishing yourself. Though your motives were undoubtedly good—you wanted to be one with *Yahweh* again—such prayers often become a way of trying to persuade *Yahweh* to love you, instead of resting in the confidence that He does love you."

"That helps me feel a little better." Asher shivered a little in the cool night air, burrowing under Papa's arm. "I'm cold."

"Here, let me warm you up." Papa reached into the tent, pulling out his mantle that was folded by the doorway. "This should help." He wrapped the dark outer robe around Asher's small shoulders. Then he paused, looking down at him. "You know, a mantle is a good illustration of this blanket of shame. Imagine if my mantle were a dirty, smelly rag. Would you want it wrapped around you?"

ASSURANCE

"Only if I were *really* cold!" Asher replied with a little giggle, wrinkling his nose in disgust at the thought.

"Nobody likes feeling defiled and dirty, like you have been feeling ever since you stole the knife. But when we have sinned, there is only one way to get rid of the dirtiness. We can't scrub ourselves clean of sin. We must confess and repent, so *Yahweh* can cover us with a new, white robe of righteousness." Papa paused. "*Yahweh* calls to your heart, saying, 'Come to Me! Let Me take your dirty robe and make you clean. That is the message of guilt. It convicts you that you are dirty, but it gives you hope of becoming clean."

"Shame also makes me feel like I am dirty." Asher squinted up at Papa in the soft light from the cloud overhead. "So the difference is, shame tells me there is no hope?"

"That's right." Papa adjusted the blanket to cover Asher's bare feet and his own. "Shame has the opposite effect. It does not draw you toward *Yahweh* with your longing for cleansing. Instead, shame drives you away from *Yahweh*. It convinces you that not even the blood of the sacrifice can cover sins as bad as yours. Shame is a lie from the enemy—a lie about *Yahweh* Himself. It is the enemy's accusation that He is not love, or that He doesn't love you enough—that you aren't worth that much to Him."

"Then I guess I can tell which one I am feeling—guilt or shame—by whether it gives me hope, or makes me feel hopeless?" Papa's words sparked a glimmer of hope in Asher's heart. But he still felt confused. "Shame made me feel like I had to pray more. If praying won't restore my relationship with *Yahweh*, then what can I do?"

"Oh, prayer is still the answer," Papa reassured him. "But you must pray in faith, not in doubt. Trust the love of *Yahweh* for you. Let your prayers be expressions of faith. Pray in gratefulness and praise, not in desperation trying to convince Him to love you. Instead, thank Him for already loving you, for covering you with grace, for restoring your relationship. Just as the Mercy Seat covers the Ten Commandments, *Yahweh* in His great mercy seeks to cover your transgression of His law. Loving-kindness—the character of *Yahweh*—is the perfect combination of justice and mercy. As you grasp how He has covered your law-breaking by His mercy, you will come to realize the greatness of His sacrifice in restoring relationship with you."

Papa shifted in his seat, pulling Asher onto his lap. "*Yahweh* wants you to trust in His love, just like you trust in mine. You cannot truly love Him with all your heart unless you believe in His love for you. Only love awakens love. You must not try to make up for your sins, to atone for them, by your own good works—by punishing yourself. *Yahweh* has torn the tree of sin from your heart by the roots. If you seek to atone for your sin by good works, you reach down into the hole and plant the seed for the next cycle of sin. When you are tempted, your heart will be easily persuaded that you can atone for it next time, too. Righteousness—having a right relationship between yourself and *Yahweh*—comes only by faith in His loving sacrifice."

"Only by faith," Asher repeated slowly. "So, I must believe in the promise of forgiveness, no matter how I feel. And when my feelings tempt me to doubt I am forgiven, I must pray in faith. I must thank *Yahweh* for His love and forgiveness until it feels real to my heart."

"Yes!" Papa answered. "And faith comes from listening to and believing the words of *Yahweh*."

"Faith is hard for me," Asher confessed. "Right after Cotton died, I felt better. But now my feelings are lying to me about *Yahweh's* forgiveness. How can I trust Him more, instead of trusting my feelings?"

Papa smiled gently. "Asher, do you remember how you felt the night of the first Passover?"

Asher's mind flitted back to the thrilling, terrifying day before they had left Egypt. After so many plagues had already happened exactly as Moses warned, everyone knew better than to doubt. What *Yahweh* said always happened! Firstborn sons whispered in wide-eyed horror about their possible fate. They watched in relief as their fathers dipped flowering sprigs of hyssop in the blood of Passover lambs, and then painted their doorposts with the blood. Asher and Iru had stood side-by-side watching their fathers, wanting to be sure nothing was forgotten.

"Yes, Papa," he whispered. "I remember." The excitement of packing and preparing, the thrill of visiting his favorite spot by the creek with Iru one last time, daring to hope that the next day they would be gone—all of these things he would never forget. But most of all, he remembered the intensity of his fear. "I was so afraid I would die."

ASSURANCE

"Do you remember when your fear went away?" Papa murmured, snuggling him close.

"Yes. It was when you painted the doorposts with the blood. When I saw it, I ran inside. I knew I was safe in our house."

Papa ruffled Asher's hair. "I remember the look of relief on your face as you raced in through the doorway!"

Asher giggled in spite of himself. "I didn't want to go back outside that whole day, not even for a minute!"

"The reason you felt safe in our home that night was because you had faith in the blood of the lamb, my son. You trusted we had followed *Yahweh's* commands, so you were covered."

Asher pondered Papa's words. "You're right. I didn't feel scared anymore after that."

"Do you see? That's why *Yahweh* has given us the Sanctuary. He wants us to trust the promises He has written into the Sanctuary service—promises our eyes can see acted out in the ceremonies using the blood of the lamb." Papa's arm tightened around Asher. "If we have faith in His promises, we trust what He says instead of what we feel—and eventually our feelings may follow."

Just like the blood on the doorposts, thought Asher. *Cotton's blood is covering me now. I am no longer under the death penalty for the sinful choices I made. Yahweh never lies! I simply have to trust His promises.* Asher lifted his eyes to the gentle glow of glory radiating from the Sanctuary. *Cotton's blood is there,* he thought. *It has carried my sin there with it. I'm safe.*

Asher felt peace melting into his heart. By faith, he could choose to trust *Yahweh's* promise that he was clean. *Yahweh, thank You that Your power and Your sacrifice set me free.* As he prayed those words, tears stung his eyes again, but this time they were tears of gratefulness. Picturing the symbols of the Sanctuary in his mind was helping him feel the assurance of being forgiven and washed clean.

How would the Messiah someday wash away all of his sins forever? Asher wasn't sure he would ever understand all of it. But as he and Papa tiptoed back into the tent, he felt at peace. He snuggled into his bed and turned to face the Sanctuary. He peered through the tent flaps at the familiar glow of the Shekinah light from the Most Holy Place.

Yahweh, You are with me again. Thank You. Thank You for covering me with the blood and giving me a new beginning. His heart warmed with assurance. He would not trust his feelings. He would trust the promise.

THINKING ABOUT IT

- What changed for Asher when he saw the blood painted on the doorposts of his house? How was his peace of mind a result of faith?

- Does God want us to live in constant anxiety or fear, wondering if we are right with Him?

- Which one comes from God—a sense of guilt, or a sense of shame? How can we tell the difference between guilt and shame?

CHAPTER 11

Judgment

Asher sat up, breathing in a deep whiff of frying manna cakes. *I must have overslept,* he thought, looking at the sunshine streaming into the tent between open flaps. He tiptoed to the doorway hesitantly, afraid to face his first day without Cotton.

"He's awake!" Zara announced as Asher peered out between the tent flaps.

Mama didn't answer, but stepped to the doorway to give Asher a warm hug. "I hope we didn't wake you. Zara and I gathered the manna this morning again. You needed the extra sleep."

Zara looked up from where she was carefully plucking a cluster of dry, brown coriander seeds from a plant in one of Mama's herb pots. "Look—Mama said we can have coriander in our manna this morning!"

"Judgment day is here!" Papa smiled. "Asher has been redeemed. We must celebrate!"

"But—isn't the day of judgment a day to be afraid?" The words flew out of Asher's mouth.

Papa looked at him, startled. "Why do you say that?"

Asher glanced over to see surprise written on Mama's face as well. "I remember back in Egypt," he tried to explain. "People talked about being judged when they died. It sounded terrifying."

Papa's strong, callused hand closed over Asher's. He hesitated, as if searching for words. "Oh, my son. Apparently we have not talked with you enough about the beauty of *Yahweh's* judgment. The judgment is how *Yahweh* saves His people! It is all about delivering us, not destroying us. This is one of the many reasons *Yahweh* wanted to lead us away from Egypt—because our understanding of Him was becoming polluted by Egyptian religions. *Egyptian* gods," his voice dropped lower, "are *nothing* like our beloved *Yahweh*."

"I used to talk about judgment often with one of my Egyptian friends before we left." Mama sighed, taking the small bowl of coriander seeds from Zara's hand. "It was so hard for her to understand. I hardly knew how to begin to explain why *Yahweh's* judgment is joyful! She lived in constant fear of death, because of the punishment that she feared might follow. The Egyptians feel no relationship with their gods, except for being scared of their power. They believe that when they die, if they can't prove their innocence, the gods will judge them harshly and condemn them."

Mama poured the tiny, round coriander seeds into her mortar bowl and ground them against its walls with her stone pestle. "The Egyptians do not believe their gods love them or want a relationship with them. They are only concerned with power, or at best, with justice—and are not always even faithful to that."

"But isn't *Yahweh* concerned with justice too?" Zara crouched by the fire. She was watching the manna cakes carefully to keep them from burning. "If we do wrong, don't we need to be scared, too?"

"Yes, but only if we refuse to confess and forsake our sin," Papa said. "It's natural for sinners to be afraid of condemnation. Adam and Eve were terrified when they realized *Yahweh* knew about their rebellious actions! But that was because their hearts had not yet changed or repented."

Papa smiled. "They didn't realize that *Yahweh's* character is the perfect combination of justice and mercy. They didn't understand that the judgment is *Yahweh* doing everything in His power to save them from justice through His mercy."

"*Yahweh* is a relational God who loves us," Mama added. "This is why we are so very, very different—our beliefs aren't like any of the nations around us. When *Yahweh* judges, He doesn't simply decide who is saved or lost. He focuses all of His energy on doing everything He possibly can, to save us!"

Papa patted the ground, inviting Asher to sit by him. "*Yahweh* wants to be close to us—just like I love to be close to you. His entire law is about relationships—with Him, and with others. He loves being connected with us, in the center of our hearts just like the

Sanctuary in the middle of our camp. He wants us to be connected with Him and others by love. That is the entire focus of His law."

"But when the Egyptians talked about judgment, it was always about fearing eternal destruction or torture," Asher said, snuggling close to Papa. "Even their sacrifices were just to keep their gods from getting mad at them. I guess I thought that since we make sacrifices too, judgment must be scary."

"Not at all," Papa assured him. "We don't make sacrifices to defend ourselves from a god who wants to destroy us. Just the opposite! *Yahweh* is never against us like the Egyptian gods. Instead, He wants to save us no matter how much pain it costs Him."

"Judgment still sounds scary to me," Zara admitted. "I guess I learned more from the Egyptian religion than I thought."

"The Canaanites and many other religions believe similarly." Mama sprinkled the dry, brown coriander powder into the smooth gravy bubbling in a pot over the fire. She pursed her lips in thought. "I suppose it is natural for humans to invent beliefs where we are either safe without letting go of our sins, or we save ourselves by doing good works."

"If that is the way we naturally think, how can we overcome it?" Asher asked.

"By faith," Papa assured him. "We trust *Yahweh's* character of love. We talk with Him every day and spend time thinking about what He teaches us in the Sanctuary. This helps us remember that He is always for us, *never* against us."

"Asher," Mama asked, stirring the manna gravy, "when I weed my herb pots, do I try to kill my plants or save them?"

Asher laughed. "You'd do anything to save those plants! You guard them like babies. I remember how you shouted at Daisy to stop her when she wandered over and nibbled one of them."

"These plants are the only things I saved from my garden in Egypt," Mama reminded him. "I trade their seeds and leaves for milk and other valuables. If they died, I'd have to beg for plants from someone else. I might never be able to replace them!"

"How is that like the judgment?" Asher asked. "You mean *Yahweh* is doing everything possible to save us, since He loves us so much?"

"Yes, exactly!" Mama stirred the gravy, then lifted a spoonful to her lips. She blew softly to cool it for tasting. "When I water my little garden pots every day, that is like the judgment. When I watch their leaves for bugs and do everything within my power to keep them alive—that is also like the judgment. I am not trying to decide which of my plants to save and which to destroy. They are all precious to me! I do everything in my power to preserve their lives."

"And that's not even a tiny glimmer compared to how priceless we are to *Yahweh*," Papa added. "The judgment is *Yahweh* doing everything possible to save His treasures—to keep us alive for eternity, living in love with Him and each other."

"That's *nothing* like the Egyptian gods." Zara's forehead wrinkled. "They didn't care about anybody."

"My Egyptian friend constantly worried she would die without enough money to buy a *Book of the Dead*," Mama said sadly. "She believed that if she were buried without at least a few pages of it in a box with her body, she would be destroyed eternally."

Mama tasted the gravy and reached for the honey. "And that wasn't all. If her family did not get her body mummified correctly, for example, she would be doomed." Mama shook her head. "If she couldn't defend herself in the afterlife and convince the gods she was innocent, she thought her gods would feed her to a monster—something like a cross between a crocodile and a hippopotamus—even if she had lived a good life."

"I'm so glad we worship *Yahweh*, and not the Egyptian or Canaanite gods." Papa smiled at Asher. "Mama did her best to tell her friend about *Yahweh*, and we hope she will not forget what Mama shared, even though we are gone. It is much easier for us to remember, though. Our Sanctuary service, the cloud above us, and even our manna and water from the rock remind us every day that *Yahweh* loves and protects us."

"The morning and evening sacrifice also remind us every day that not one of us is perfect yet," Mama pointed out. "We are covered by grace every day! We are constantly assured that every person who surrenders and repents is safe. The morning and evening sacrifices remind us every day that we have new chances to grow in love."

"Judgment is all about saving you." Papa smiled as he reached over to tap the tip of Zara's upturned nose. "It's not scary—it's a reason for rejoicing! Judgment is simply *Yahweh's* process to deliver us from punishment. His great purpose is to defend us from the accuser—to set us free."

"Why does the accuser always want to destroy us?" Zara's brown face clouded with anger. "It seems like he is always trying to make us live in fear!"

"You're right, Zara," Papa said grimly. "But in the story of Joseph, do you remember what happened to his accuser?"

"Do you mean Potiphar's wife?" Asher scowled. "I suppose she thought she got away with her wrongdoing. But in the end, Joseph was proved innocent!" Asher beamed, recalling the ending to his favorite story. "She must have felt foolish when Joseph ruled all of Egypt. I bet she never saw *that* coming!"

"I bet she didn't!" Papa's laugh rang out in the clear morning air. "That's an excellent example of the judgment. In our world, injustice often seems to win temporarily. But *Yahweh* promises to make all things right in the end. Through the judgment, He declares us righteous despite our past mistakes, because He covers them with the sacrifices. This is called vindication. Not because we are perfect," he cautioned, "but because He is righteous. Because of the Messiah's sacrifice, any guilty person who repents will become innocent. They are vindicated—like Joseph."

"*Yahweh* rules with true justice. He never condemns anyone whose heart has been cleared of sin," Mama declared, heaping steaming manna cakes onto plates and handing them to Papa, Asher, and Zara. "The judgment is all about salvation, vindication, and deliverance," she added. "The only people who should be scared in the judgment are the ones who keep on breaking relationship with *Yahweh* and others by putting themselves first. The judgment is *Yahweh's* doorway to an eternity of peace and love after the Messiah comes. Unlike the gods of other religions, *Yahweh* is never against us!"

JUDGMENT

"And that sort of judgment," Papa grinned as he poured coriander-speckled gravy over his manna cakes, "is something to celebrate!"

THINKING ABOUT IT

· How did the Egyptians feel about judgment? Was their salvation based on faith in the love of their gods, or on their own actions?

· Did God want His people to be afraid of judgment, or relieved to know He was working through the judgment to set them free?

· Does it make you happy to know God is judging you—doing everything He can to vindicate, save, and deliver you—right now?

CHAPTER 12

The Feast

"Mama," Asher asked one sunny morning as he swept leaves and loose pebbles from near the door of the tent, "will I ever see Cotton again?"

His mother stood from the pile of bedding she had been rolling up just inside the tent. "That's a good question, Asher, one for which I do not have an answer from the writings of Moses," she admitted. She walked over to Asher, laid her hands on his shoulders, and looked into his eyes. "But this I know: *Yahweh* our Creator put so much love in your heart for little Cotton. We know someday He will make all things right. He will reward good and punish evil." She brushed the curls from Asher's forehead. "Messiah will come, and He will make everything beautiful. He will wipe away all tears. I cannot imagine He will allow you to suffer for all of eternity with the pain of Cotton's loss."

Mama smiled as she returned to her work, and Asher joined her in rolling sheepskins. "Cotton did no evil, either," she assured him. "In fact, he was one of *Yahweh's* best examples, showing you how Messiah would come someday to rescue you from your sins. Cotton helped you to understand that the judgment is all about *Yahweh* doing everything He can to rescue and save you. If it will make you happier to have Cotton with you for eternity," she smiled, reaching over to wipe a tear from the corner of Asher's eye, "I'm sure He will find a way to restore him to you."

Asher piled the last sheepskin roll in the corner and gratefully wrapped his arms around his mother's waist. "Thank you! I can't wait for Messiah to come. I can't wait until there is no more death or sin or suffering—and everything is at peace again—because at-one-ment will be finished!"

Over the past month, Asher had slowly adjusted to the loss of his pet. Daisy looked lonely at first, but Mama had sold some of her beautiful handmade woven cloth to a neighbor and bought an orphaned black lamb for Asher. Daisy and the new lamb, who Asher named Eden, cavorted around the bushes and stones as merrily as Daisy and Cotton once had.

Eden's soft black wool would someday become a robe for him, but even now, her affectionate nuzzles warmed his heart and softened his sense of loss. He would never forget Cotton, but life would go on. Now Asher looked forward to the Day of Atonement as never before.

The week before the Day of Atonement was busy. In the ten days leading up to the special day, Mama and Zara washed all their clothing and blankets and scoured every pot, dish, and lamp they owned. Asher and Papa gathered wood, hauled extra water, and scrubbed heavier things. There was an atmosphere of excitement in the camp as the holy day approached.

Most importantly, people took time for heart preparation. They took walks alone to pray and think. If there were any sins to be confessed with sacrifices at the Sanctuary, they should be confessed beforehand. The Day of Atonement was a day to live in the sight of a holy God without intercession for any deliberate, known sins. Though the

---

[1] Numbers 28:3-4; 29:7-11

morning and evening sacrifices still covered daily mistakes on the Day of Atonement, all intentional sins should be confessed beforehand so they could be washed away by the sacrifice that day.

Friends stopped by often to chat and ask forgiveness, making sure any misunderstandings or hurt feelings from the year had been mended. Unresolved tensions healed and relationships grew and were refreshed.

Asher especially enjoyed when friends with children his age stopped by to see Mama and Papa. In the evenings, they laughed and talked in the soft light of the cloud overhead, sharing stories and news. It felt so good to know that no one was separated by resentment or misunderstanding.

For the first time, Asher was more eager for the Day of Atonement than he was for the feast that came first. This year, he felt like he had crossed an invisible line separating childhood from adulthood. This year he understood why the Day of Atonement was so important. How comforting it was to know his sins no longer rested on his own shoulders! They were already in the Holy Place, waiting. Tomorrow, they would be washed away forever! He couldn't imagine how he would feel if he hadn't already confessed and repented of his stealing and lying. The thought made him shudder.

The morning before the Day of Atonement, people woke early to gather manna for the special feast that would take place before sunset. The camp buzzed with anticipation. After breakfast, women and girls rushed to bathe in their part of the river, while men and boys hurried to their own area. Everyone dressed in clean, fresh robes.

Mama and Zara giggled excitedly as they taste-tested the warm manna cakes that afternoon. They had added zesty dried berries and honey they'd saved for weeks just for this occasion. Mama helped Zara sprinkle the manna cakes with precious cinnamon brought from Egypt. They were always grateful for the manna, a daily reminder of how *Yahweh* lovingly provided for them. But it was wonderful to have a new flavor for a change!

Nervously, Asher ducked inside the tent for a quick look around to be sure everything was clean and in order. Iru's family would be arriving for supper any minute.

THE FEAST

"Hello, Joshua!" At the sound of Iru's father's voice, Asher's heart leaped with dread. *What if Iru won't even talk to me?*

"Peace to you, Caleb!" Papa's warm voice rang out. "Come, join me by our table stone! What a blessing it is for our families to be together for the Day of Atonement feast."

Asher wanted to hide in the back of the tent, but he swallowed hard and forced himself outside into the afternoon sunshine. Surely anything was better than waiting.

Iru stood beside his father, scuffing his toes in the dirt. "Hi," he mumbled to Asher. "How are you?"

"Good," Asher's voice was a hoarse whisper instead of the cheerful greeting he intended. He forced himself to smile despite the pounding in his chest. "And you?"

"Glad it's almost suppertime." A hesitant smile played around the corners of Iru's mouth.

"Me too. I'd better help Mama bring out the rest of the dishes." Asher turned and rushed back toward the tent, almost smacking into his mother in his haste. *Could have been worse,* he thought.

During supper, each time Asher glanced over at Iru, his face flushed hot with embarrassment. Though Iru had said he had forgiven Asher, he sensed Iru didn't want to be around him anymore. Asher sat on a mat on one side of the circle of people, and Iru on the other side, making no effort to join Asher as usual. *I can understand why,* he thought miserably.

Supper was undeniably delicious. The two families chatted cheerfully, seemingly unaware of the boys' discomfort. When Iru came back to the flat stone table for a second helping of manna, Asher mustered up courage and joined him. *Please, Yahweh, help me,* he prayed.

"How's your manna?" Asher asked Iru hesitantly. "I love the cinnamon."

"I like cinnamon, too," Iru muttered, vigorously stirring the bowl of manna pudding his mother had brought. "It—it reminds me of Egypt." He stood beside Asher for a moment in awkward silence before moving toward the other side of the circle to sit down again.

Asher sighed. The heaviness of their broken friendship continued, a sobering reminder of what had been lost. But at least they were together. Their families hadn't given up. It was, after all, almost the Day of Atonement. *At-one-ment.* He wrapped the thought around himself like a comforting blanket. *Yahweh wants all of us to live in at-one-ment, with Him and with others,* he thought.

A burst of loud laughter and shouting from a nearby tent interrupted Asher's troubled thoughts. He caught Zara's gaze as her wide eyes darted from the other tent to the adults seated on smooth stones and mats nearby. She frowned. "Did they forget tomorrow is Day of Atonement?"

"Hush, Zara," Mama reproved gently. She rose and then sat down beside her daughter, smoothing her curls. "We cannot read other people's hearts."

"Shouldn't they be celebrating the feast, though?" Asher asked in a more subdued tone.

"Well, not everyone welcomes Day of Atonement the same way," Mama admitted. "Some people don't feast. And unfortunately, some in the camp don't pay much attention at all to what *Yahweh* has told us to do. They seem to feel they are at peace with *Yahweh* without even searching their hearts."

Asher pondered for a moment. "Well, are they?"

"Are they what?"

"Right with *Yahweh*. I mean, what if we don't search our hearts? Are we still covered by the morning and evening sacrifices? Or are we on the wrong side, then?"

"The boy asks good questions, Joshua." Iru's father grinned at Papa.

"Endlessly!" Papa chuckled, then turned to Asher. "First, this is not a question we can answer for others. We cannot know what is in their hearts, so it is not safe or wise for me to venture a guess as to whether our neighbors are in right relationship with *Yahweh*. All we can know for sure about others is that *Yahweh* is doing everything He possibly can to judge them—meaning, to save them and to win their hearts to love Him. You boys already know that the judgment is beautiful because *Yahweh* wants to save every person. Our task is to give our own hearts entirely to *Yahweh* every moment of every day."

"How can we know our hearts are right?" Iru's voice came from the other side of the circle.

"That question must be for you, Caleb," Papa chuckled, beaming at Iru's father. "It seems our sons are beginning to ask the questions of adulthood!"

"The morning and evening sacrifices are given by *Yahweh* to remind us twice a day to search our hearts for any way in which we have forgotten to love Him and others." Iru's father's deep voice boomed from the other side of the fire pit. "The sacrifices do not automatically cover people who are not living with repentant hearts. Even if their sins seem small—like complaining or disobedience—there is no such thing as a small sin. But again, we must remember—we cannot know where they stand with *Yahweh*."

"We are not even good at reading our own hearts," Mama pointed out. "Perhaps the best way to know whether our hearts are pure is to ask ourselves where our thoughts go naturally. What topics do we find most interesting in conversation? How do we like to spend our free time after our work is done? To whom or what do we devote our warmest affection?" She patted her son's head. "These things show us who has our hearts. It is best if we focus on searching our own hearts, rather than attempting to figure out where others stand with *Yahweh*."

"We know the law is all about relationships," reminded Iru's mother. "We are supposed to love *Yahweh* with all of our hearts. But it can be hard to know whether we do truly love Him. Often, we see hints that we love Him well when we ask Him to show us any way we are seeking to control others instead of loving them, or letting bitterness or distance grow between ourselves and others."

Asher glanced at Iru, but Iru's eyes were fixed on a dark, distant hillside.

The two families ate and talked in front of the tent until sunset. As dusk fell over the camp, the ram's horn sounded for the evening sacrifice. Conversation hushed in reverence.

"Let's sing," Mama suggested. Iru's father began a psalm. Children and adults joined in worshipful harmony. They sang for half an hour in the twilight. The glow from the distant Sanctuary burned gradually more brilliant as the shadows deepened.

"It's time to pray," Papa said at last. Under the radiance of the pillar of fire overhead, they knelt facing the Sanctuary. From the oldest down to little Elah, each one prayed.

"*Yahweh*," Asher whispered when it was his turn to pray, "thank You for making our hearts clean again. Thank You that our sins will be washed away from the Sanctuary tomorrow. Thank You for at-one-ment."

When he looked up after prayer, Iru's eyes finally met his.

THINKING ABOUT IT

- Why did God want His people to clean everything in their households before the Day of Atonement?

- How did God want the Day of Atonement to affect people's relationships with one another? With Him?

- Are there any relationships in your life in which you need to make an apology or seek healing now?

CHAPTER 13

The Day of Atonement

In the past, Asher had always dreaded the Day of Atonement because it meant fasting— no food all day long! But now for the first time, he understood the deep joy of this day. Today his sins would be washed away from the Holy Place!

Of course, morning and evening sacrifices were new beginnings for the camp every day. But today was a much more special new beginning. All the evil that had been placed in the Sanctuary during the past year would be washed away by the goat's sacrifice. This blood would cover the confessed sins represented by the blood sprinkled on the horns of the Altar of Burnt Offering in the courtyard, and before the curtain in the Holy Place, since last year's Day of Atonement. Today the Sanctuary and the camp would be purified of all the sins from the past year!

Crawling from between his sheepskin blankets, Asher peeked out the tent flap toward the Sanctuary. Already small groups of people were drifting toward the linen wall. "May I go to the Sanctuary?" he pleaded.

Papa nodded. "Stand by that corner, the one closest to the Most Holy Place," he said, pointing. "We will find you there in a little while."

Not everyone in the camp could fit easily into the huge area surrounding the Sanctuary tent at once, but Asher and his family liked to spend at least some of the day close to the Sanctuary. Part of their time would be spent quietly in silent prayer, and Asher wanted to pray now. Soon, there would be so many people it would be impossible to get close.

Asher slipped through the crowd gathered in the spot his father had pointed out. He knelt near the outer curtain. The light from inside the Sanctuary glowed brilliantly through the linen cloth in front of him. He fingered the small, spattered stain on the hem of his robe where a few drops of Cotton's blood had fallen. He thought of the other part of Cotton's blood, carried in the priest's bowl to the horns of the Altar of Burnt Offering, and perhaps to the ground before the curtain in the Holy Place. *My sins are about to be washed away from the Sanctuary forever,* he thought.

As the trumpet sounded from inside the curtain fence, Asher pictured what was happening. Like always, he imagined the beautiful red, blue and purple cloth walls stretching high above his head in the Sanctuary. The golden angels woven into the fabric would gleam in the soft light of the seven candlesticks. He inhaled the rich, bittersweet incense smoke and visualized it drifting thick and billowing inside the tent.

How beautiful it must be! He imagined his prayers, carried symbolically in the smoke floating up, up, over the veil into the Most Holy Place, where *Yahweh's* glory blazed above the Mercy Seat of the Ark of the Covenant. *Hear my prayers now,* he pleaded earnestly. *Make my heart pure. Show me if there is any sin in me, so that today I can be at peace with You, and my sin will be gone forever!*

The usual morning sacrifice had already been made by now, covering all of the accidental and less significant sins committed since the evening sacrifice at sunset. Anyone who had confessed and repented would be cleansed. *Yahweh's grace is so abundant, so freely offered to anyone who turns away from sin and chooses to live righteously,* Asher thought. *He is so good!* Contemplating this daily sacrifice brought him comforting assurance, and he bowed his head to pray. *Surely, You are as eager to be close to me today as I am to be close to You,* he prayed. Though he knew in some ways *Yahweh* could only dwell in the blazing light in the Most Holy Place, Asher was beginning to understand the deep and personal relationship *Yahweh* longed to have with His people.

Since Cotton's death, Asher had prayed regularly as he herded the sheep and went about his daily chores. He had a constant sense of his Creator's power and love now, and longed for intimate closeness with the One who understood how hard it had been to sacrifice Cotton. Someday, somehow, he realized that *Yahweh* was going to make a similar sacrifice in love, to cover his sins and wash them away forever.

Though he could not see it, Asher knew that two goats would soon be taken before the High Priest. One goat would be chosen by a special process to become the Lord's goat. The other would become Azazel (uh-ZA-zel), the goat sent into the wilderness. There would be a sacrifice to cover High Priest Aaron and his family. The process of sacrifices would take a few hours. In his heart, hopefully alongside the rest of Israel, he and his family would think quietly about the meaning of the ceremonies.

The rest of the year, priests brought the blood only to the horns of the altar or into the Holy Place, sprinkling it before the veil. No one entered the Most Holy Place where the Ark of the Covenant stood. But today was different. Today, High Priest Aaron would sacrifice the Lord's goat. Then he would go into the Most Holy Place with this goat's blood and sprinkle it before the Mercy Seat of the Ark of the Covenant. This blood would cover the sins already represented in the courtyard and Holy Place by sacrifices all year long. Sins that had already been confessed and repented would now be washed away forever.

"Hi, Asher."

Asher jumped in surprise and turned toward the familiar voice. "Oh! Hi, Iru!"

Iru sat down beside him, his face sober. Asher felt a rush of fresh sadness over what he had done. He wasn't sure where to look or what to say. He lowered his head and dug his fingers into the dirt between them, sifting for small stones.

"Your papa said I could find you here."

Asher lifted his eyes. "You *wanted* to find me?"

"Sure." Iru shrugged and looked toward the Sanctuary. "I mean, I know I didn't talk to you much last night. I wanted to, but it's hard to talk about things with everybody there."

"I thought you never wanted to talk to me again," Asher muttered, looking down at his dusty fingers.

"Well..." Iru picked at a blade of grass. "I didn't, at first. I was mad. I mean, you knew how sad I was about losing my knife, but you didn't tell me you had it. I didn't understand why you were so mean."

Asher sighed. "I can't explain. I felt really bad sometimes, but then I didn't know how I could tell you after it had been so long. I didn't want to make up more lies to cover it up, so..." he trailed off miserably. "I guess sin always makes everything a mess. I don't know what to say. I'm just really sorry now."

"I know." Iru turned toward him. "I could see how sad you looked last night at supper. As much as I was upset about my knife, I realized last night your friendship means a lot more to me than a knife. After all," he said, rolling a rounded pebble between his fingers, "knives don't last forever. Friendships do. Or at least, they're supposed to."

Asher stared down at the dirt. He wasn't sure he dared to hope for Iru's friendship again—not after everything that had happened.

"That's what the Day of Atonement is all about—being close to *Yahweh* and others," Iru said. "And I realized last night I'm not doing my part. I've stayed angry at you, and it's been pushing us apart. Can—can you forgive me?"

Asher glanced at his friend's face. Iru's usually cheerful expression was clouded with sadness. Had he heard correctly? Iru wanted *his* forgiveness? "But I'm the one who messed up," he said. "I deserve for you to be mad me."

"Your sin separated us at first," Iru said softly. "But that doesn't make it okay for me to let my sin separate us now. As my papa says, wrongdoing is always rooted in wrong relationships. I haven't loved you very well. You've confessed and repented. I don't want the Day of Atonement to pass without us having at-one-ment."

"I don't feel like I deserve your forgiveness," Asher said, his chest feeling tight. "But I forgive you for being mad at me. That's the least I can do."

"Then we are both covered by the atonement. Cotton's blood covered your sin; mine is covered by the morning and evening sacrifice today." Iru grinned at Asher. "We have a new beginning!"

"That's what the Day of Atonement and all of the Sanctuary service is about," Asher beamed back. "New beginnings!"

THE DAY OF ATONEMENT

"By the way," Iru added, "will you teach me how to whittle with my knife? I'm not very good at it, but I would like to learn. Maybe you can meet me at our swimming hole later this week?"

Asher heaved a sigh of relief. "I'd love to!"

THINKING ABOUT IT

·   What did the Day of Atonement change for the entire camp?

·   How does seeing our own sinfulness help us to forgive others who sin against us?

·   Restoring trust after we do wrong is difficult. How can we help others believe we are trustworthy again after we have sinned against them?

CHAPTER 14

Finally Free

"There they are!" Asher spotted Zara and Elah darting toward them, with Papa and Mama following behind as their eyes scanned the crowd. Iru's parents walked beside Papa and Mama.

"Over here!" Iru shouted, waving.

Asher scrambled up from his spot on the ground beside Iru and pressed through the crowd. He slipped his hand into Papa's. Iru wove through the throngs of people to his father's side, and their family moved toward the other corner of the Sanctuary. Iru looked back and waved.

Asher waved back with a grin. *Forgiveness.* It felt so good to be at peace again. *Thank You for at-one-ment!* He couldn't stop smiling as he breathed a silent prayer toward the Sanctuary.

"When will they sacrifice the Lord's goat, Papa?" Zara asked. Asher felt a twinge of sadness at the thought of the goat being sacrificed exactly where he had put his hands on precious Cotton's little head.

"Sometime in the next hour, I think," Papa said.

Mama wrapped her arm around Asher's shoulders. "Soon," she whispered, smiling down at him. Asher realized Mama understood his burden, too.

A murmur spread through the crowd, starting at the other end of the Sanctuary near the entrance. "Azazel! The scapegoat has been chosen!" The goat representing the evil one had been selected. This goat would be sent into the wilderness to wander alone. The scapegoat symbolized people who refused to repent, choosing to die for their own sins instead of accepting the Day of Atonement sacrifice.

A chill shot up Asher's spine. If he had not repented, he would have been represented by the Azazel goat now—responsible to take the punishment of death for his own sins because he had refused to repent. *If I had waited until today, it would have been too late to confess!* Had he not confessed, the Day of Atonement sacrifice would not have covered him now. *But I am not condemned today! I am free!* he thought, pressing close to his mother and wrapping his arms around her waist.

From inside the curtained fence, Asher heard a goat bleating loudly. The sound ended in abrupt silence. The Lord's goat had been sacrificed.

"What are they doing now?" Zara asked Papa, slipping her hand into his.

"It will take them a few moments to finish preparing the sacrifice to burn on the Altar of Burnt Offering in the courtyard," Papa said. "Since the sacrifice for High Priest Aaron's family is already done, he will now go into the Most Holy Place and sprinkle the blood for all the confessed sins waiting in the Sanctuary since last year's Day of Atonement."

It seemed to take forever, but finally Asher heard it—the soft, beautiful tinkling of the bells on the hem of High Priest Aaron's robe as he strode slowly into the Holy Place on the other side of the Sanctuary's curtain walls. All was silent for a few moments. Asher realized the High Priest was probably standing still in the Holy Place for a final prayer.

The gentle tinkling of the bells on High Priest Aaron's robe resumed, moving closer until Asher felt sure he must be in the Most Holy Place. Asher closed his eyes and breathed in the heavy scent of incense. *Yahweh, my sins are before Your throne now. Wipe them out forever, please!* He heard the rhythm of High Priest Aaron's bells pause again, and imagined the white-haired priest standing in the blazing glory of the Most Holy Place before the Ark.

After a pause, the bells began to jingle softly again, moving farther away as High Priest Aaron walked back out of the Most Holy Place. Asher opened his eyes, suddenly realizing he'd been holding his breath.

He wasn't the only one. A great hush had fallen over the whole crowd around him. Now smiles of joy brightened all of the waiting faces. Mama wiped away tears. Everyone rejoiced, embracing one another. Someone began singing a psalm, and everyone else joined in.

The atonement was complete! All sins that had been confessed and brought to the Sanctuary before the Day of Atonement were now washed away! *Yahweh* and those who were surrendered to Him were in at-one-ment, at peace. What a glorious day! *Thank you,* Asher prayed, gazing first toward the Shekinah glory blazing from the Sanctuary, and then at the sky. *Thank you, Yahweh, for taking away my sin.*

"Perfect surrender means perfect peace," Mama whispered. She brushed a strand of curls from Zara's forehead.

"When we trust *Yahweh's* love," Papa said, "we love Him back—and then His love pours through us, and we love others."

"Iru came to talk with me," Asher beamed at Papa. "Thank you for telling him where to find me!" Papa gave him a squeeze. Asher felt warm all over. Papa understood.

At home that evening, Asher and Zara knelt on the mat in front of the tent with Papa and Mama to pray as the ram's horn blew for the evening sacrifice. *Even on the Day of Atonement,* Asher realized, *there are still ways we have not perfectly obeyed the law of Yahweh to love Him and others. We have more to learn every day about loving well. And yet, Yahweh accepts and loves us just as we are.* His heart warmed with the comforting thought that on the Day of Atonement, just like every other day, grace covered every repentant sinner in the morning and evening sacrifices.

FINALLY FREE

As if echoing his thoughts, Papa leaned over and wrapped his arm around Asher's shoulders. "Even today, we need the morning and evening sacrifices. The Day of Atonement is, more than any other day of the year, a day of grace."

Mama smiled at Zara snuggled beside her, then pulled her onto her lap. "Today and every day, *Yahweh* is judging us—doing everything He possibly can to vindicate us, to save us, to set us free from sin and condemnation. When we prayerfully meditate on His grace, we grow to love Him and others more every day."

"Today I realized how sinful I am," Asher said soberly. "I could have been doomed like the Azazel goat. Even though I am clean of my sin of stealing Iru's knife and lying about it, I have often broken relationship with *Yahweh* and others by complaining or cherishing selfish attitudes in my heart." He paused. "I also realized the Sanctuary service is really all about *Yahweh* giving us new beginnings. Every sacrifice is a new beginning."

"Someday, at the end of earthly time, *Yahweh* will finish His loving judgment work, uniting everyone in love." Mama smiled and squeezed sleepy Zara. She smoothed her soft cheek, and Zara's eyelids closed sleepily. "To restore at-one-ment to the whole universe, sin must be destroyed, along with those who love sin instead of loving *Yahweh*. But from now until then, the freedom and beauty of the Sanctuary is the most important message we can share with people around us."

Papa nodded. "*Yahweh*, like the ram Abraham found on the mountain, offers Himself as a sacrifice in our place to save us from sin."

Asher smiled at his little sister cuddled sleepily in Mama's lap. "This year, I want to celebrate my new beginnings by being more thoughtful to Zara, to both of you, and to others outside our family."

"That's the spirit of at-one-ment, my son," Papa said proudly. "Your words come from a heart surrendered to *Yahweh*—ready to serve Him and others out of love. When our hearts are filled with love, we seek to do what He says instead of following our feelings. By faith we obey the law of love, even when it is painful. By faith, we let *Yahweh* help us respond in love to every situation."

SANCTUARY LIGHT

THINKING ABOUT IT

- Why was there a morning and evening sacrifice, even on the Day of Atonement?

- Why does perfect surrender mean perfect peace?

- How would things be different in your family and home if all of your actions were guided by love to God and others?

CHAPTER 15

Perfect Peace

"I'll race you to the top!" Asher shouted to Zara, as he dashed toward the winding path up the mountainside.

"No fair! You started first!" Zara pouted, turning back to walk beside Mama.

Mama smiled and clasped her small hand. "I love having you walk with me."

Papa strode up the narrow trail in front of Mama and Zara. "Looks like you'll have to wait for us if you want to hike together," he called after Asher. "And look what I found here!" Papa squatted in the shade of a boulder, cradling a delicate pink desert flower in his rough, work-worn hand. Mama and Zara knelt to sniff and exclaim over the fragrant blossom. Reluctantly, Asher trotted back to admire the flower before resuming his dash up the rocky slope.

An hour later, Asher collapsed on the wide, flat stone at the top of the mountain trail. Zara dashed the last few steps to join him. Together they laughed as they flopped down on the warm surface to rest. After catching their breath for a few moments, they sat up to gaze down into the valley. From up here, the tiny people walking among the tents looked like ants. Giggling, they pointed here and there, trying to identify the figures far below.

"Your growing legs are too fast for me!" Papa joked, as he and Mama reached the flat stone and sat down beside them, panting. "But of course, you didn't have anything to carry." He reached into his pack and drew out a leather bag of manna cakes for their picnic. "And I bet those legs won't take off to explore anywhere when we open these."

Mama unrolled a woven bulrush mat on the flat stone. Then she leaned against a rock and gulped gratefully from the goatskin water jug. "I've been looking forward to this for at least half an hour."

"Can we eat? I'm starving!" Asher begged.

"Let's pray," Papa smiled. "Thank You for our food, and for covering our sins today," he prayed. Then Mama began handing out manna cakes.

"I've been so careful today," Zara bubbled. "Is it possible I haven't even sinned at all? I really want to be perfect for *Yahweh*."

Mama smiled and handed her a manna cake. "It makes me so happy to hear how your heart longs to please *Yahweh*! And in one way, it is always possible to be perfect. We can always be—should always be—perfectly surrendered."

"If we are perfectly surrendered," Asher reflected, "are we fully obeying *Yahweh's* law?"

"The simple answer is . . . yes and no," Papa said. "We can be free from sins that we know, but still be doing sinful things that do not bring us under the condemnation of *Yahweh*."

"How is that even possible?" Asher bit into his crispy manna cake. "Doesn't sin always bring punishment and condemnation?"

"Not necessarily. Only those who know to do good, and don't do it, are under condemnation." Papa gazed out over the valley for a few moments in silence. "That's part of why *Yahweh* calls for the morning and evening sacrifice in our encampment.

Unknown sins are covered if we are surrendered to Him in love. Our goal is much higher than perfect behavior. It is perfect surrender."

"What's the difference?" Zara asked.

"That's a great question!" Papa's eyes twinkled. "Maybe I can explain it this way. What was our goal in coming on this family hike?"

"Getting to the top of the mountain, of course!" Zara giggled. "I love it up here on the stone. Especially when the wind blows through my hair! It feels wonnnnderful!" She stood up and spun around, laughing, before collapsing at Papa's feet again.

"Reaching the summit is a good feeling," Papa laughed. "And thinking about that goal helps us keep climbing. But if our focus were only on reaching the end of the trail, wouldn't we miss out on the joys of the hike? We might easily forget that we came on this hike to spend time together as a family, to focus on loving *Yahweh* and others. Then we wouldn't take any time to examine little flowers, pretty stones or other beautiful things along the way that remind us of *Yahweh's* love. We might even concentrate our efforts on beating each other to the top." He winked at Asher, who ducked his head and grinned guiltily. "The purpose of our hike is to grow in love for *Yahweh* and each other—not just to reach the mountaintop." He looked down at the children. "Do you see the difference?"

"I think so," Asher said.

"I don't," Zara's lips puckered in a tight frown. "Do you mean if we think too much about reaching perfection, we can't be perfectly loving?"

"*Yahweh's* goal is more about the journey than the destination," Mama explained. "Our purpose in life is to learn to love *Yahweh*, and to love others as much as we love ourselves. Thinking too much about becoming perfect someday in the future could distract us from learning to love right now, where we are."

"*Yahweh* is the perfect expression of love. And our focus must always be on becoming like Him," Papa added. He opened the goatskin water jug and took a long drink, then passed it on to Asher and Zara. "So in that sense, we are always seeking to reach the end goal of becoming perfect! Keeping our eyes on Him, our 'mountaintop,' keeps us on the narrow way that leads to life."

"I get it!" Asher's eyes lighted up with excitement. He wiped manna crumbs from his chin as he reached eagerly for another manna cake. "Keeping our eyes on *Yahweh's* perfect love helps us want to become perfectly like Him someday. But it also helps us to love Him and others now, every day!"

"Yes!" Papa beamed. "When we love Him and others, obedience to His law of love is the natural response from our surrendered hearts. Just like sin is always a heart issue, obedience is also always a heart issue."

"Some people define sin as behavior," Mama said. "They try to make rules for their families that will prevent anyone from accidentally breaking any laws. It seems like a good idea, and their hearts are sincere!" She shifted her sitting position on the hard stone. "But thinking of sin as just things we *do*, and making rules so we can stop doing bad things, easily leads us to rely on ourselves. We look down in scorn on others who decide on different rules. We begin to think we can stop sinning just by trying hard enough. Or we feel like we are being good without *Yahweh's* help if we follow all of the rules. We forget our hearts are still selfish. Hearts do not change just by following rules about behaviors."

"Is that why when I promise myself I will be perfect all day, even though I try really hard, I always seem to forget?" Zara asked.

"Yes. And again, that's why *Yahweh* gave us the morning and evening sacrifices," Mama said, "to help us realize that even if we haven't done something bad on purpose, our daily mistakes that break the law of love still need to be covered by grace." She smiled. "Sin is rooted in attitudes of selfishness. Selfishness always starts with a cycle of unbelief and pride. Sinful behaviors are merely the fruits of the seeds of unbelief and pride growing in our hearts."

"What do you mean by a cycle of unbelief and pride?" Zara asked.

"All sin starts with unbelief," Mama said. "The first act of the enemy was to doubt the loving character of *Yahweh*. But the moment he questioned *Yahweh's* love, he also became prideful. By disbelieving *Yahweh*, he was basically saying that if *he* were ruling the universe, he would rule better than *Yahweh*."

"Later, Eve's first sin was also doubting *Yahweh's* love," Papa added. "The moment she started to believe that *Yahweh* was selfishly exalting Himself above her, she began wanting to exalt herself too." Papa reached for another manna cake. "Every sin since then has been rooted in the same cycle. When we choose unbelief in *Yahweh's* unselfish love, the next step is prideful self-exaltation."

"So if the cycle at the heart of all sin is unbelief and pride," Asher said slowly, "then the cycle at the heart of all righteousness must be faith and humility."

"You are growing wiser by the day, my son." Papa ruffled Asher's curls. "That's exactly what I was going to say! As we believe more and more in *Yahweh's* love for us, we grow in our love for Him. Because He loves us, He never puts Himself first, but always gives Himself as a servant. He sacrifices Himself for us. The more we realize that, the easier it is for us to unselfishly serve each other."

"I think I can show you an illustration of that," Mama said, gathering up the manna bag and pointing to the woven mat she had placed on the stone under their food. "Zara, do you remember when we made this mat from the bulrushes we gathered from the Nile River?"

"Oh yes!" Zara giggled. "That day was fun. I got to wade in the mud. Carrying the pile of rushes home was hard, though. They were heavy!"

"Yes, they were!" Mama laughed. "But now they are dry and lightweight, and they aren't in a pile. What holds these leaves together?" Mama asked, brushing her fingers over the intertwined bulrush leaves in the mat.

Zara flopped on her stomach to examine the mat, and she and Asher studied the weaving. "I guess they are holding each other," Zara said. "They go over and under each other. That's how they all stay together."

"Yes," Mama said. "But what is happening in this corner?" Her fingers brushed over a ragged edge.

"They can't hold onto each other anymore there." Asher picked at one dry leaf and peered underneath. "The rope around the edge is coming off."

"That rope is just like the love of *Yahweh* holding us together," Mama said. "Each of us is called to be like these bulrush leaves. We go under each other in order to hold one another up. Each one takes its turn going under the others, and the others take their turns being the one underneath. As each one goes under the others, together they become a mat instead of a useless pile of leaves."

"The rope border holds it all together," Zara marveled, examining the twisted cord of bulrush fibers around the edge. "No rope, no mat!"

"Aha!" Asher said. "The rope around the edge is like *Yahweh's* love. Are you saying we can't let go of our selfishness and put others above ourselves, unless we trust His love to hold us up in the end?"

"Exactly!" Mama beamed. "This is the law of love that holds together the universe. Each bulrush leaf is like a person who chooses to lift others up instead of exalting himself or herself. We can only let go of the higher place and raise others up if we trust that, even if we don't push ourselves to the top, *Yahweh* will hold us up Himself."

"Faith in *Yahweh's* love is the way He helps us love others!" Zara exclaimed. "When we trust His love, we love Him back, and we love others. We don't have to fight for our pride, so we can let go of the highest place."

"I get it!" Asher shouted. "That's how our hearts change our behavior. The more we trust in *Yahweh's* love for us, the more we naturally love others instead of fighting for what we want. That's how faith and humility become a cycle of righteousness!"

"Yes! It's really the opposite of trying to get *Yahweh* to love us by behaving well," Papa said. "That's why rules can't change our hearts—only loving surrender does. Trying to achieve perfect behavior someday can distract us from our goal every moment—*perfect surrender.* If I am perfectly surrendered to *Yahweh*, I am perfect *right now*—even though I still need to learn to love better every day."

Mama stood up and dusted manna crumbs from her robe. "Perfect surrender is possible every moment. That's what makes it a much better goal than achieving perfect behavior someday. In perfect surrender we find perfect peace. Like a plant, we may be perfect at every moment, and yet have infinite room to grow more in learning to love *Yahweh* and others."

"If we want to become perfect someday," Papa said, "the best way to get there is to practice entire surrender today and every day." He stood up to wrap his arm around Mama's waist. "That's why *Yahweh* gives us opportunities to learn to practice His perfect love in our families and our other relationships constantly."

"Come over here with me," Mama invited, taking Papa's hand and walking over to the edge of the stony overlook, where the camp stretched far below them into the distance. "I want to show you something."

Asher and Zara scrambled up from their seats on the stone. Together they gazed out over the vast encampment sprawled below them in the valley. Thousands of tents in neat rows made a rough square across the sandy plain between the craggy desert mountains. In the middle of the square, the Sanctuary tent stood alone in a large empty space. With its covering of dark animal skins, it looked tiny and plain inside the rectangle fence of fluttering white linen curtains around it.

"Do you see how small and insignificant the Sanctuary looks from here?" Mama asked. "Like everything else about the Sanctuary, I believe this is a symbol of how Messiah will appear. He will not seek to exalt Himself. Like a lamb, He will sacrifice Himself, taking the lowest place so that we may be lifted up. Perhaps this is the central message of the Sanctuary—that *Yahweh* always takes the lowest and humblest place, in order to lift us up. Like the tent in the middle of the camp, *Yahweh* wants to be one with us. The more we have faith in His humility, the more we will become like Him, humbling ourselves and lifting others up."

"That is the reason *Yahweh* is safe to rule from the throne of the universe." Papa's dark eyes shone with love. "He can be trusted to have that power, because He is entirely empty of the thirst for power. This is the essence of His character. This is what love means—never, ever exalting self."

"As we become like Him, our lives are guided more every day by the power of love, instead of the love of power." Mama smiled tenderly at Asher and Zara. "We don't want to lift ourselves above others anymore, because we see how *Yahweh* always does what is best for the people He loves, instead of for Himself. This is our goal every day—to learn to trust *Yahweh's* unselfish love more."

"Can you see why righteousness—right doing—flows naturally from faith?" Papa asked. "Only by love is love awakened. We must have unshakable confidence that *Yahweh* is always for us, never against us! Instead of exalting Himself, He always lifts us up. The more we believe in *Yahweh's* self-sacrifice for us, the easier it becomes to sacrifice for Him, and to surrender self for the good of others around us."

"Someday, at the end of earthly time, *Yahweh* will finish His loving judgment work. He will bring at-one-ment between Himself and all people who surrender their hearts to Him,"

SANCTUARY LIGHT

Mama smiled, hugging Papa as the whole family looked out over the plain. "Someday, the universe will be united in love. Sin and anyone who loves and cherishes sin in their hearts must someday be destroyed! The whole universe will be woven together in loving, self-sacrificing relationship. But until then, the message of the Sanctuary is the most important message the world can ever hear. It is the message of *Yahweh's* unimaginable love—of judgment that leads to that final at-one-ment." She smoothed Asher's curls and stroked Zara's smooth cheek. "Everyone needs to know that *Yahweh* puts Himself on the altar as a sacrifice, in order to save us from sin, come close to us, and teach us how to love Him and one another."

"I love *Yahweh*." Zara whispered. "I want to love Him more every day of my life."

Asher's eyes turned toward the dark, simple-looking Sanctuary. His heart throbbed with warmth and peace. "I love *Yahweh* too. How could anyone resist that kind of love?" He looked up at Papa. "Thank you for teaching us these things, Papa. I'm so thankful we can learn about His love and grace in the Sanctuary."

"Me too, my son," Papa whispered, pulling him close. "Me too."

THINKING ABOUT IT

· How does unbelief in God's unselfish love tempt us to self-exaltation and pride?

· How does faith in God's self-sacrificing love help us become humble and loving toward Him and others?

· What will you remember best as the message of the Sanctuary?

THE END

CONCLUSION

The Israelite Sanctuary was the worship center to which God's people eagerly streamed at least three times per year (Exodus 23:14-17), as it was their light and hope. In that sacred location, worshipers found forgiveness and the assurance of God's presence and salvation, received new courage to live, and strength to struggle with the difficulties of life. Peace and joy accompanied the Sanctuary's activities. Going to the Temple of God was a solemn occasion; and on their way, the people would sing (see, for example, Psalms 120-134). This was the place where people wanted to be; they longed for its presence (Psalm 42-43). King David even wanted to stay in God's Temple all his life in order to gaze upon the beauty of the Lord, searching for His truth, experiencing His goodness, and seeing His face (Psalm 27: 4, 8, 13). One day in the house of Lord was better than a thousand elsewhere (Psalm 84:10).

The doctrine of the Sanctuary is a foundation and central pillar of Adventist faith. It is summary, essence, and core of our theology, and brings together

CONCLUSION

"a complete system of truth" well "connected and harmonious" (Ellen G. White, *The Great Controversy*, p. 423). Our pioneers recognized the power of this teaching, because it gravitates around Jesus, unifies biblical teaching and comforts believers. This truth empowers God's people to focus on and fulfill their mission.

The Sanctuary services together with the festivals were object lessons about the Gospel. It was a master plan explaining the process of salvation. The whole plan of redemption was captured through them, presenting a big drama about God—who He is and what He is doing—revealing His abhorrent attitude toward sin and His abounding love for people. They tangibly demonstrated how God saves people and that there is no future for unrepentant sinners. The God of the Sanctuary is the God of love, truth, and justice. His holiness permeates everything, and sin has no place in His Presence. The services performed in the Sanctuary demonstrate that God is in charge and the ultimate Victor in the great controversy between good and evil, truth and lie, light and darkness. Satan is defeated. This victory was won on the cross and is unfolded more and more until the full display occurs when sin and those who choose to associate with it will be no more.

The Lord of the Sanctuary is the God of deliverance and freedom; He is the re-Creator. The beautiful display of God's actions on our behalf in the Sanctuary brings assurance into our lives and teaches us that God can indeed be trusted. We can build and cultivate a meaningful and joyful relationship with such a trustworthy God. As our High Priest, he does everything possible to save us. He blots away our sins and gives eternal life. All these are His actions, never our achievements. He lives with those who are humble and contrite in their heart (Isaiah 57:15; 66:2; cf. Psalm

CONCLUSION

51:17). He is smiling on us not only to create a large smile on our faces, but through us to bring smiles into lives of many other people. God wants us to live such a happy, abundant and satisfying life (John 10:10) that it will produce growth in His grace and our usefulness.

Understanding how God's people celebrated festivals in the past and how they worshiped God in the Sanctuary with all its different sacrifices help us to recognize that the life of God's church in Old Testament times was God-centered, because all these events were focused on God. This teaches us that also our life and worship need to be always God-centered. Paul aptly states: "So whether you eat or drink or whatever you do, do it all for the glory of God" (1 Corinthians 10:31 NIV).

— Dr. Jiří Moskala, Dean of the Seminary at Andrews University and Professor of Old Testament Exegesis and Theology

WAFERS MADE WITH HONEY

1 c. water
½ c. oil
½ c. honey
1 tsp. salt
4 c. flour (whole wheat or white, or some mixture of the two)
2 tsp. coriander, cinnamon, or anything else desired for flavor (optional)

Combine water, oil, honey, salt and any flavorings or spices in bowl and mix. Add flour and knead into a soft dough. If dough remains sticky, add a little more flour until it is smooth and does not stick to fingers. If it is too tough to be easily molded with fingers, add a little water.

Roll dough flat, about ¼ inch thick. Cut with a knife or cookie cutters. If desired, dough can be molded into shapes, but make sure it is not too thick, so the center will be cooked thoroughly before the thinner edges/ends get burned.

Baking Option:
Bake at 350 Fahrenheit (175 Celsius) for 15-20 minutes (depending on thickness of dough) on a greased cookie sheet or baking stone.

Frying Option:
In a small amount of oil, fry dough in small patties about ¼ inch thick, over low/medium heat. They should look similar to pancakes.

Serves about 4.

GLUTEN-FREE WAFERS MADE WITH HONEY

1/3 c. olive oil
1/3 c. honey
2 c. oat, brown rice, or sorghum flour
1 ½ tsp. coriander, cinnamon, or anything else desired for flavor (optional)
¼ teaspoon salt

In small bowl, beat together first two ingredients with fork. In another bowl, stir together remaining ingredients. Pour liquid into dry ingredients and mix together well. Flatten dough on cookie sheet, then cover with plastic wrap and roll out further. Cut with knife or cookie cutters. Bake at 350 Fahrenheit (175 Celsius) for 8 minutes or until lightly toasted in color.

Serves about 4.

Made in the USA
Columbia, SC
13 October 2020